MASK OFF
Two Faces

PRECIOUS D. DAMAS

MASK OFF

Two Faces

Precious D. Damas

Redemption's Story Publishing, LLC, Harlem, GA (USA)

Precious D. Damas

Mask Off:
Two Faces

Print ISBN 13: 978-1-948853-61-3
Digital ISBN 13: 978-1-948853-62-0
Library of Congress Control Number: 2023900544
Printed in the United States of America

This is a work of fiction. Names, characters, businesses, events, and
incidents are the products of the author's imagination. Any resemblance to
actual persons, living or dead, or actual events is purely coincidental.

Content Warning. **BE ADVISED:** This book contains the use of strong
language and adult scenes. Readers under the age of 18 are discouraged
from indulging due to its potentially influential nature.

For information and bulk ordering, contact:
Redemption's Story Publishing, LLC
P.O. Box 639
Harlem, GA 30814
RedeemedByHim@Redemptions-Story.com

Dedications

I would like to dedicate this book to my sister, the late **Belinda Ann Jackson**, whom I miss dearly. There's not a day that goes by that I do not think of her and wish she were still here with us. Belinda was amazing and IS a great listener! What do I mean? I still talk to her, and I know she is still listening to my every word. I remember the day she told me, *"When I am gone, I want you to live your life. Do what you enjoy – and do it well."* I love you, Nookie, and I miss you like crazy! Until we meet again…

I dedicate this book to my daughter as well. Thank you for believing in me when I brought this to your attention and asked for your help. You started me off, and I soared with it! Three series later! Can you believe it? You're the best teacher I know, a good person, and a great mother! Thank you for your input, advice, thoughts, and vision!

To my beautiful grandchildren: This is for you, too! Thank you for making me smile and laugh every time I see your faces. When it's raining and grey outside, you all make my day shine brightly when I see or even think of you. I can't wait to see you grow from your little people's bodies into your adolescent bodies, into your teen bodies, and then into your can't-tell-me-nothing bodies. Remember always: Puma loves each and every one of you!

Lastly, I give a special dedication to my nephew, the late Elijah Corey Jackson. For many years, I walked around here tough as nails and showed everyone what "strong" looks like. You were the one who let me know it is okay to be weak. My heart broke the day you left me. I now know what it feels like to sleep with a broken heart. I wish I could have done more to see your pain. Lord knows I would have been there all the more for you. I know how much you loved me because you told me every time we talked. I also know you knew how much I loved you in return. To this day, know that I still love you, and I am okay. Love Your Auntie O'Really Swoom.

Acknowledgments

I would like to acknowledge my mother, who birthed and cared for me to the best of her ability. I look at her daily and think to myself, *"If it was not her…if it weren't for her struggles…if it weren't for her endless love and support…if it weren't for her addictions…if it wasn't for her going through what she went through to show me, 'I AIN'T ABOUT THIS LIFE! I DON'T WANT THIS LIFE!', I wouldn't be the person I am today."* Thank you, Ma! I miss you so much and can't wait to see you again! May you continue to R.I.H.

I would also like to acknowledge my husband, who met me at a time in my life when I was not in a "good place." Even though we ran around like we were Bonnie and Clyde, he showed me the finer things in life. Let's just say I was spoiled and never wanted for anything! After 35 years of being together, three beautiful children, and six beautiful grandchildren, what more can I ask for? I love you!

To my children, who have always told me to do something just for me. I would often start off doing just that and end up doing it for them. Leavens, Jr., you are the apple of my eye. You are so laid back and protective of others, even down to the bugs. You are the most kind-hearted person I know. I realized that the day you saw me crying when you were around one or two years old. I recall you scooting next to me and saying, *"Mama,"* all while hugging me tightly. From that day forward, I vowed you would never see me cry again. Strong became all I knew!

Le'Vaughn, my "what goes around, comes around" child! You gave me a run for my money (and are still taking my money to this day)! It was either your way or no way. You've always been clever, spontaneous, and very bright. I remember when I brought you home from the hospital and laid you on the bed so we could take a nap. I also recall being very careful not to squish you while resting — but when I woke up, you were right under me with your eyes wide open. I immediately jumped, thinking I may have hurt you, but you were okay. Until this day, I ponder, *"How did he squirm his way over to me like that?!"*

Lastly, to all my family and friends not mentioned here by name: Thank you **ALL** for your love and support!

***** *LET'S GO!* *****

To My Editor and Publisher

I want to acknowledge Angela Edwards, Editor and Publisher Extraordinaire. The world would be a better place if we all would stop and say thank you to the people who stood by you when you took flight. It's beautiful when people give their time to mentor, educate, and uplift you from start to finish. Angela, your support means everything to me. Without your patience, support, and understanding, I couldn't have made this happen. I gave you my story, you saw my vision, and then said, *"Let's do it!"* Well, I did it! It's done and ready!

So, thank you for your mentoring and for picking up the phone when I had those late-night questions. Most importantly, thank you for being there for me through my difficult times.

Respectfully Yours,

Precious Damas

Preface

Where do I begin? Well, if you know me, then you already know my story. For those of you who do not yet know me, this book was inspired by the reading of another book. I thought to myself, *"I can definitely relate to this story!"*

I grew up in a good family with morals, values, and a bunch of strong women. I enjoyed my childhood...until the crack epidemic reared its ugly head and took some good people down whom I loved. It then became survival mode for me and a host of other young people. I did like many others at the time: I tried to make a dollar out of fifteen cents by selling weed. I did many "things" during that time in my life, but I never degraded myself or lowered my standards. Instead, I learned my lesson — and here we are today!

One day, I asked God to give me a path on which to walk. He led me to it, and I began the journey. In the beginning, I kept asking Him for directions due to me having no real sense of direction to begin with. I went back and forth, scratching my head and biting my bottom lip in a state of utter confusion. Then, God spoke. *"Let **Me** show you your life."* From that day on, my writing journey gained its foothold on that path.

It is my sincerest hope and prayer that you will get to know me and a bit about my life through this story and that you enjoy it from beginning to end. It is said that everyone has a gift waiting to be unwrapped and used. This is my gift to you. If I must say so, I've read many books in my day...and this is one of the best ever by far!

From the bottom of my heart, thank you ALL for investing in me!

~ PDB ~

Introduction

This will be brief because I want you to dig right into the meat of the story.

Mask Off is a riveting tale of money, revenge, and love. The main character, Saint, will make sure she delivers on all of the above. You will see some people get hurt, while others become "attached." Some people will walk away, while others will rest where they lay.

In the end, there will only be one winner who will walk away with it all:

MONEY

PEACE

AND

LOVE!

Table of Contents

Chapter One

The nearness of summer could be felt in the air. The date is Wednesday, May 24, 1995. Saint is lying in her bed, looking up at the ceiling in deep thought. She is still in complete shock about how the day before, both of her brothers were sentenced to 15 years in prison! As if that weren't bad enough, her twin brother was gunned down within two years of all this drama. Saint cried softly in the confines of her room, just like she did in the John Adams courtroom in Boston as the judge said, "This will be the last time you two brothers will terrorize the streets of Boston for many years. You will serve no less than 15 years in the Walpole Penitentiary!" That day was the last time she hugged and kissed her brothers for a very long time because the next time would be behind plexiglass and talking to them on the phone. She remembered her eldest brother Sharmel handing her a letter in the courtroom that she had yet to read.

As Saint remained lying in bed, she reminisced on old times when her family didn't have much money and lived in the Orchard Park Housing projects in the rough neighborhood of Roxbury. In the late '80s and early '90s, Orchard Park was out of control. Prostitution, drug deals, gangs, and shootings were rampant. The projects were widely known as "The

Territory for All Evil." After her father's death, her brother Sharmel was introduced to "the game."

Their father was murdered on his way home after the late-night shift at the Chocolate Factory in Lower Mills Milton. Their father was the man who made the chocolate at the factory. Saint loved it when he came home from work because he always had some chocolatey goodies for them!

Saint recalled the day her father didn't come home…

~~~~1989~~~~

At 7:46 a.m., I heard a loud, hard knock on the front door, followed by my mama screaming and crying uncontrollably. I leaped out of bed and ran into the living room. There stood two Boston Homicide Detectives. The Black detective's nametag read, "Detective Derek Williams." The White detective's nametag read, "Detective Shawn Connolly." Both wore button-down shirts with ties, slacks, and shiny dress shoes. Covering their shirts were jackets that read "Boston Police Homicide."

Hot on my heels were my brothers. They ran out of their bedroom and stopped at my side. We stood in the living room in a state of **SHOCK** at the sight of our mama on the floor in hysterics.

"Mama, what happened?" I asked as tears began to flow from my eyes. I knew something was wrong…something was about to change our lives forever. *"Please, mama! **Answer me!**"*

Detective Williams replied, *"I am sorry to have to tell you this, but your father was robbed for his wallet and murdered at Ashmont Station this morning."*

I returned my attention to our mama, still on the floor screaming, crying, and praying aloud. I then turned to Sharmel, Shein, and Rein. They were stone-faced. I could see the wheels turning as they thought about revenge. I just couldn't understand how someone could murder our father! He was a hardworking man who loved his family.

You know how people say that someone was simply at the wrong place at the wrong time? Well, I don't believe that shit! My father was where he was supposed to be — at Ashmont Station, waiting for the bus to bring him home to us…to his **FAMILY**! I think about my father every day because he never received the justice he deserved.

~~~~~~~~~~

The room's silence was broken when Saint said softly, *"Daddy, I will never forget you. I love you."*

Saint recalled how, after her father's death, Sharmel became a different person. He took the role of "the man of the house" very seriously and quickly stepped in as the breadwinner for our family. He met an "OG" (Old Gangster) named Shadow. Everybody in Boston knew who Shadow was, as his reputation preceded him. He was an older man, tall and dark-skinned with a low fade. His car of choice was a blue 1968 Cadillac Deville. Shadow was on a mission to get someone under his wing, but he needed that person to be loyal and trustworthy because his goal was to train them to take over "the game."

Shadow heard about Sharmel from some of his boys. They spoke highly of her brother because he didn't run with anyone but himself. At the time, he was only selling weed, but that was for the lightweights in "the game." Although he knew that, he also knew it was bringing home more money than any 9-5 job he could have ever worked.

Saint remembered the day she was hanging outside with her best friend Monae on the stairs, keeping a watchful eye on Sharmel posted up at the park with his friends. Suddenly, Shadow pulled up, yelled something out the window to the group, and then Sharmel got up and climbed into the car. Monae and I looked at each other with concern because we knew nobody ever got close to Shadow. In an instant, Shadow's car sped away with her brother inside, going only God knew where.

Later that night, Sharmel returned home with a suitcase. At the time, Saint had no idea what the hell was in it but came to learn it was bricks of cocaine. A few years later, Shadow was gunned down while sitting in his car—a tragic incident that Sharmel took very hard because, after our father's death, Shadow became his father figure.

After Shadow's death, Sharmel knew it was his time to rise and become the King of Boston. He needed a loyal and trustworthy crew, though. Shein and Rein approached their older brother and expressed interest in joining "the game." Sharmel hesitated at first because he didn't want them involved, but with their insistence, Sharmel finally agreed.

Sharmel, Shein, and Rein ran the streets of Boston. They were unstoppable and virtually untouchable. Sharmel's right-hand man was a dude named Mykal. His time was relatively short-lived because he was shot soon after Sharmel and Rein's sentencing. No one had heard from him since.

You know how they say once you are gone, you are gone forever? Well, Mykal was about to return—and the streets better be ready!

Sharmel had a new connection in Miami named Zion. Whenever Sharmel needed some bricks, Zion was his go-to man. Zion was a lot like Shadow: you could never get close to the guy, but he was always there when needed. Sharmel was cool with that arrangement because he understood. He was that type of dude, too.

~~~~~~~~~~

Shit was about to come to a halt the day one of the twins was gunned down by one of their enemies. It all started when Saint's twin brother Shein met up with some chick in the summer of '92 named Unique. She was the quiet type but very up-to-date on what happened in the hood. She knew all the gossip, like who was dating, who had the nicest car, and who had the deepest pockets. That broad even knew who had the biggest cock. Unique was a young thang—a freshman in high school and her mother's only child. She got whatever she wanted from her mother and rocked all the latest Adidas sweatsuits, matching shell-toe Adidas sneakers, Kangol hats, and bamboo earrings, and her hair was always on point.

Unique was always fascinated by the ballers' lifestyle and wanted a taste of what it was like to be a baller's girl. Little did she know it wouldn't be as glamorous as she had envisioned all those years. Because she lived a very sheltered life, the closest she ever got to a baller was watching the movie "Scarface" over and over again. She was only 16 years old, and her mother had a tight rope around her arm. Wherever you saw her mother, you saw Unique. Many people thought they were sisters!

Unique's mother knew what it was like on the streets in the Bean. By the age of 16, she was prostituting herself and hooked on cocaine. She birthed Unique when she was 19 years old, which was a blessing because it prompted her to clean up her act with the quickness. Because of her past, she did whatever she could to protect her baby, but the ballers were Unique's drug—and she was hooked!

Shein met Unique at the Pit Stop on Morton Street. He slipped his phone number into her pocket, and they were inseparable from that first phone call. Shein would only talk to her on the phone, when her mom was at work, or when she went to Che'vou. Che'vou was the skating rink where all the kids would hang out on weekends. That went on for a year until Shein asked Unique's mother if he could date her daughter, to which she agreed.

As their relationship grew serious, Shein spoiled his prize girl. He bought her everything she wanted and more, ensuring that she had nothing but the latest and best shit. When Sharmel suggested that Shein ease up on his spending habits, Unique caught wind of it and didn't like it at all. She was just like all the other gold-digging females, and she was not having it! "If I don't get it from Shein, I'll get it elsewhere," she thought.

In direct response to the mere threat of Shein taking a chill pill on spoiling her, Unique started going to the skating rink without him — often. She started running with some chicks from a different crew who lived on the other side of town, where they had their own ballers.

One thing about the Bean that was widely known was that everyone stayed on their side of town, making their own money. The only time a crew came to another crew's side of town was either to see one of their baby mamas or to retaliate for an injustice to one of their own. The Handsome Brothers — Sharmel, Shein, and Rein — ran Dorchester, Mattapan, Roxbury, and Hyde Park. They were trying to take over the South End, but the Italians had that on lock. They even paid some of the police to turn a blind eye to their illegal activities in the streets!

Unique was on a mission. She started messing around with some kid named Ricardo from East Boston. Ricardo had everything on lock on his end of town. He ran East Boston, Chelsea, Lynn, and Malden. He wasn't as big as the Handsome Brothers, but he had a little something going on for the Spanish part of town. The Handsome Brothers weren't sweating Spanish Ricardo because they had big money. They could easily take over his part of town if they wanted to.

Things took a turn for the worse when Shen found out that Unique had been messing with Ricardo for about a month. He also found out she was three months pregnant and decided to have an abortion. Shein's blood was boiling! "Don't sweat her, man," Sharmel warned, but Shein didn't listen. He hunted her ass down, beat the shit out of her, and left her badly bruised and beaten. When Ricardo heard about it, he was ready for immediate revenge. That's when it all came to a halt.

The Friday night after the assault on Unique, everyone was down at Club Spot, enjoying the night. It seemed like anyone who was someone was out that night. People came from everywhere because Lady Saw and Beenie Man were in town. Due to the club being full, they were not letting any more people into the club that night, so the party continued in the parking lot. No one was leaving. Meanwhile, Sharmel, Shein, Rein, and the rest of their soldiers were inside having a good time. Unique ended up getting in because she was with Ricardo and his crew. Sharmel sensed something wasn't right as he observed Ricardo not enjoying himself. He followed Ricardo's glare, which was directly on Shein. After a few moments of uneasiness, Sharmel signaled to his brothers that it was time to bounce. Something wasn't right in the atmosphere.

Sharmel, his brothers, and their soldiers departed the building, but they didn't notice Ricardo and his crew had already exited first. As Sharmel and the others walked outside, they had no idea their lives were going to change right before their eyes.

BOOM! BOOM!

Two gunshots rang out. Everybody scattered in every direction to take cover. Sharmel called out for Shein and Rein.

He didn't really give a fuck about his soldiers at that moment. He knew if anything ever happened to either of his brothers, he could never forgive himself. Rein answered him. Shein didn't. He had been shot two times in the chest and died right on the spot. That was another tragic loss to senseless violence for the Handsome family.

Ms. Handsome couldn't even cry. She did all the crying she could when she lost her husband. After his death, she decided that all she would do was pray and make sure her only daughter made something of her life.

After Shein's funeral, Sharmel and Rein took a break for a while. They needed to clear their heads and figure out what their next move would be. They weren't about that "retaliation life"; they were about making that money.

Three weeks after Shein's funeral, word on the streets was that the remaining Handsome Brothers put a hit out on Ricardo. That was the word on the streets, but the real talk was that someone had snitched on them about being drug lords.

Sharmel and Rein hired some of the most prominent attorneys in the industry to work on their case: a five-man team of elite professionals. The detectives were on their job. They had photos, surveillance, and audio. Before they knew what hit them, the Handsome Brothers went down — caught by the law. The brothers were looking at 30 years in prison, but their attorneys worked their asses off and got each brother only 15 years.

~~~~~~~~~~

Saint cried some more as she thought about her life without her brothers' presence. She knew things would be different now that her brothers would be gone for a long time. She thought about Sharmel's main man Mykal. Whoever shot him nearly took off half his damn face! The funny thing about the whole situation was that he was taken to the hospital, and no one had seen him since. It's almost like he disappeared off the face of the earth. Besides our brothers, Mykal was the only other person Sharmel trusted with his life.

Saint sighed, jumped out of bed, dried her tears, and went downstairs to greet her mother. She walked straight into the kitchen because she knew her mother would be there cooking breakfast and singing her favorite hymn, "Amazing Grace."

"*Good morning, baby! I've cooked turkey bacon, scrambled eggs with cheddar cheese, and buttermilk pancakes. I know they're your favorite, sweetie,*" her mother said with a broad smile.

Saint replied softly, "*Thanks, Mama. I love you.*"

The ladies sat at the kitchen table and talked about life. Both knew things were going to be a lot different for them. They knew they still had each other and that their old life was behind them, although still a present memory. They discussed how grateful they were to live in a $1.8 million home in a neighborhood called "Newton Hills." Indeed, their home was beautiful: a Victorian-style mansion with seven bedrooms and four bathrooms. Saint and her mother needed a fresh start, far away from their old neighborhood.

After eating breakfast with her mother, Saint retreated to her room to finally read the letter Sharmel had written to her.

~~~~~~~~~~

Dear Saint,

I don't even know where to begin with this letter. I first want to apologize to you and Mama because I never wanted to hurt either of you. My intentions were to give you the life you both deserved. After Papa passed away, I became the man of the house, and I felt as the man of the house, I was supposed to be the provider and protector. I needed fast cash, so when the opportunity came knocking, I jumped quickly without any hesitation. The money started coming so fast, I got hooked on its flavor! The next thing I knew, I was running Boston. I had everything on lock. I had the power, the money, and got the respect! At that point, there was no turning back. My biggest regret is that I brought Shein and Rein down with me. I should've encouraged them to do something better with their lives, but they wanted to be men, too. I understood what they were going through because I wanted to be a man when I was their age. For that, I am truly sorry.

Saint, I gifted you something nice: ownership of the six brownstone houses in the ATL. You will find everything you need if you check in the guestroom's vanity. I know what you are thinking right now. **"What the hell, Sharmel?!"** *Don't worry, baby girl. I got you. I am working on putting something together for you so that you can sell the brownstones.*

I will call you Thursday around 4:00 p.m. I will also keep writing to keep you posted on the plan I have set up for you.

Remember: I will always love you. Please take care of Mama and let her know I love her, too!

Until pen and paper meet again…Sharmel

~~~~~~~~~~

Saint sat on the edge of her bed, shaking her head in disbelief. All this shit was too much for her to deal with right now. She knew she had to be strong for her mother because they only had each other. *"What the hell does Sharmel have planned for me? **I'm no drug dealer!**"* she thought to herself. All she could do was wait until she received the promised call from Sharmel.

~~~~~~~~~~

Thursday morning, Saint tuned her 65-inch flat-screen Sony TV to Fox 25 News. Cindy Fitzgibbon was reporting on the day's forecast: a balmy 82 degrees. *"Perfect weather!"* Saint exclaimed. *"Not too hot, and definitely not too cold."* She turned off the TV, entered her private bathroom (which was in her bedroom), showered, and brushed her teeth. When she exited, she strolled into her walk-in closet. The space was full of designer jeans, shirts, dresses, shoes, sneakers, boots, accessories, and so much more. Her outfit of choice for the day was a grey Juicy Couture jumpsuit and white Nike Air Force Ones. She dressed quickly, grabbed her book bag, and rushed downstairs to the living room to say goodbye to her mother. Her mother was seated in her favorite chair, reading the Bible—

one of her daily activities. *"Bye, Mama! I'll see you later. I love you!"*

"Bye, baby! I hope you learn something good in class today. I'll have dinner waiting. I love you, too!" her mother replied as Saint rushed out the door to get to class on time.

Saint jumped into her cherry red Range Rover HSE, fully equipped with Italian leather. She had Mary J. Blige's "My Life" CD in the first of her six-CD slots and played track number six—"My Life." She pumped up the volume and sang along with Mary as she made her way to the campus.

Saint pulled into the commuter student parking lot of Bentley University, the Waltham Campus, and parked. She jumped out and started walking to her class in the Business Management Building. She was a senior at the university, majoring in Marketing. She hoped that after graduation, she could start her own marketing business to help other companies with their marketing strategies.

As she sat in class listening to the professor's lecture for about an hour, she found her mind wondering about the 4:00 p.m. call from her brother. She was curious about his plan to help her get rid of the six brownstones. When class was finally over, Saint had some time to kill. It was only 1:30 p.m., so she drove to Newton Highland Deli for lunch—about a 20-minute drive from the school. She sat alone and ate a Chicken Caesar sandwich with chips and iced green tea. After lunch, she headed to Natick Collections Mall to kill some more time before going home to talk to Sharmel.

She drove down 128 South, blasting her Mary J. Blige. Once at the mall, she parked near Macy's. As soon as she walked into the mall, she saw the Tiffany and Co. store, so she went in and browsed their charm bracelets section. She saw one that caught her eye: a white gold bracelet that she loaded up with charms. She chose a heart charm, one that read "Mom and Dad," another with an "S" (for Sharmel), a different style "S" (for Shein), and an "R" (for Rein). Saint spent over $1,000 for that bracelet, but every piece meant something special to her. She stopped for a moment to look at her watch: 3:15. She hurriedly exited the mall, jumped into her Range Rover, and sped off.

Saint made it home at 3:50 p.m. She ran into the kitchen to greet her mother. *"Hi, Mama!"*

"Hi, Saint! How was your day?"

"My day was good. And yours?"

"It was great! I spoke with and sang to God. Now, I am cooking dinner – a honey-glazed chicken with garlic potatoes."

"That sounds really good, Mama!" Just then, the phone rang. *"Excuse me, Mama. I need to get this call."* Saint ran upstairs and answered the phone.

The operator on the other line said, *"You have a collect call from Cedar Junction at Walpole...Sharmel* (her brother's voice came through). *To accept this call, please press one. To decline the call, please hang up."*

Saint pressed one.

"Hello, Sharmel!"

"Hey, baby girl! How are you?"

"I am good, big bro! How are you?"

"I am fine. I don't have long to talk, so let me tell you what I need you to do. Go visit Majesti. You remember him, right?"

"Yes, in the ATL."

"Good. He is going to help you sell Mama's beautiful brick houses."

Saint knew how to talk in code, so she understood what her brother was truly referring to. *"Alright. When do I need to go down there?"*

"You need to leave Saturday."

"Okay. I will."

"Saint, I love you so much. You stay up, baby girl. I will write you letters while you are down there. Please tell Mama I love her. I can't talk to her yet because it causes me a lot of pain to hear her voice."

"Alright, Sharmel. I will relay the message. Please don't forget to write me. I love you, bro." Saint heard the operator state, *"You have 20 seconds."* Before she could say a formal goodbye, the call disconnected. She sat on her bed, thinking, *"**Damn!** Sharmel wants me to go all the way to the ATL with six bricks so that Majesti can help me get rid of them — and I have to leave by Saturday! Well, it's time to start planning because it looks like Mama and I are going on a vacation to the ATL!"*

Chapter Two

Back in Miami, Zion laid in a hospital bed with a mask completely covering his face. For a moment, he almost forgot where he was. His mind was consumed with thoughts concerning that last year-and-a-half and what brought him there in the first place. As he laid there, he was haunted by all the jacked-up memories, including when his right-hand man, Shein, was killed by Ricardo. *Why was his girl so damn naïve and curious that she chose to roam around in the pits of Hell with the enemy?*

After Shein was killed, it was only a matter of time before the Feds caught on to the fact that he was in the game, so they went after his brothers—Sharmel and Rein.

"Those muthafuckin' crooks! That's the shit that pisses me off. I know damn well they were getting paid in full. Where the fuck is the remorse?" thought Zion.

Zion's heart hurt for Ms. Handsome the most because she was not cut out for what went down. She lost her husband, then her son. Now, her other two boys are doing 15 years in the joint. What really messed her up was Little Saint no longer had anyone to look up to. It was just her mom and her now. Thank

God for Sharmel's wisdom before he died. He had a separate life prepared just for his mom and little sisters that the Feds couldn't touch. Everything they owned was legit. The house and businesses were untouchable.

Meanwhile, Unique's mind was so controlled by that nigga Ricardo, she forgot what side of town she lived on and what was supposed to be important to her. Before long, Zion was informed she was not doing well. She was deeply in love with Shein and had a hard time handling the fact that **she** was the cause of his murder and that he was really gone. Unique started tricking, doing all kinds of drugs, and even turned into a snitch. Zion was in complete shock when he heard *that* shit! Unique was beautiful and still had the innocence of a child, even after all she had gone through. One might've thought Shein stole her innocence — **and they would've been wrong.** He truly loved her. But that damn Ricardo? He turned her **OUT**! Word on the street was that she had contracted HIV. Her mother couldn't take it anymore, so she moved out of the state and left Unique to fend for herself.

Zion felt his blood begin to boil as he thought about Shein's demise. *"That dude, Ricardo, was the one who took my boy out. He and his crew were also the ones who tried to kill me that day Sharmel and Rein were sentenced as I was leaving the courthouse.*

Shit, they nearly took my face off! Payback is a bitch, though." He forced himself to relax before he set off all the bells and whistles of the machines he was attached to. He achieved success not a minute too soon because in walked the doctor and a nurse.

"Zion, are you awake?" the doctor asked.

"Yes, I am," came his mumbled reply. For over a year, he had been in and out of the hospital, getting surgery after surgery. Today, he was **finally** ready to get the mask off his face.

The nurse was next to speak. *"I am going to press the button to lift your bed so the doctor can remove the mask."* Zion felt the bed move but couldn't see anything at first.

"I am going to start removing the mask now, Zion," the doctor calmly stated.

He nodded his head yes, indicating that he understood, and closed his eyes. He was so anxious to see his new face. The nurse rubbed his back and spoke gently to him, saying, *"I know this is going to be very emotional for you. You have been in a very deep sleep and heavily sedated on drugs for a few days."*

In his head, Zion screamed, *"A few DAYS?!"*

Once the mask was removed and he was permitted to look in the mirror, he honestly felt like the old him. It had been five years since that punk, Ricardo, blew off his face. Zion felt good about his new look, especially since he had grown out his hair. The dreadlocks he now had fit perfectly with the fierceness of his face. He was ready to get out of that hospital to handle his business on the outside.

"Zion, I need you to follow all of these procedures carefully. Keep your head elevated and apply ice to minimize the swelling." The doctor paused briefly before continuing. *"Don't smoke or be exposed to second-hand smoke during your recovery."* The doctor noticed Zion slightly raised a questioning eyebrow. *"Finally, please take your pain meds as directed. Call or come in to see me immediately if you have any problems."*

After the medical duo left the room, Zion reached for the phone to call his aunt because he needed a ride home. For some strange reason, no one answered. *"She's probably out running errands. After all, it is Saturday,"* he said aloud to no one in particular. He had no other option, so he pressed the button for the nurse's station. When one responded, he asked her to call him a cab to take him home. Nothing in him made him want to stay there a second longer than he had to.

~~~~~~~~~~

Once home, Zion couldn't help but admire the immaculate grounds surrounding his mansion. The landscape held a maze design that spelled out the name **"BELLA."** It wasn't something one could see with the naked eye from the ground, but it was clearly outlined when viewed from the second-story balcony facing the front lawn.

He opened the door to his 2.4-acre storybook replica of a French Norman estate, walked into the kitchen, and was greeted by a stack of mail resting on his black Angola granite counter. As he flipped through the mail — **bills, bills, and more bills** — he came across a letter from Sharmel Handsome. He set aside all the other mail pieces and took the letter into the living room. He took a seat on the black Italian leather sofa and ripped open the envelope.

"My dude. He's the only one who knows where I am. Not even Rein knows," Zion mused. *"Rein was my partner, but he doesn't have much heart like his **brother**."* A smile formed on his face as he began to read:

Dear Zion,

I hope when this letter reaches you that you and your family are in the best of health. Yea, man, they fucking got me. Those muthafuckas finally got me. It's all good, though. I was facing some heavy time – 30 years – but my lawyers got that shit down to fifteen. Fuck it. I'll take it. How have you been? How's the car business? I am sure it's very successful because cats like you always make that money.

I am writing to ask you for a favor. My baby sister, Saint, is headed down to the ATL. You remember my little sister, right? Well, she's not little anymore and is quite a beautiful young woman. Dudes are steady tryin' to holla at her, but they already know she is off-limits to them. She already knows, too. Hell, I taught her well! Anyway, man, she's going to see if she can try and sell those six brownstones. Since I'm in for a while, she and MaDukes will need that money to maintain. While there, she's going to be staying with one of my ex-soldiers from back in the day. You feel me? His mom and mine are best friends, so I trust the cat. But you know the rules: You can't trust a cat too much. I need you to be my eyes, just in case dude decides to fuck up and start actin' shady. His address is 589 Ovalene Lane. I have enclosed a current picture of Saint.

Please keep your eyes open at all times. I'll be catchin' up with you.

Later, Bro. Stay up!

Sharmel

~~~~~~~~~~

Zion remained seated on the sofa in deep thought. He knew he was on a mission for his boy, so he had to put a plan into effect. As he looked at Saint's photo, he recalled the days he used to be in love with her and how Sharmel would not allow him to have a relationship with his sister. Saint was off-limits. Period.

Saint was nothing like the other girls in the hood. Just because her brothers were running shit and had money, she never let it go to her head. She was all about her education and getting out of the hood. Zion liked that about her. He remembered her asking him why he was in the game and what he got out of it — and he had no solid answer to either question. Another time, during Thanksgiving dinner at their home, she asked if he was afraid to die. Again, he was left answerless. Suddenly, out of nowhere, she gave him the softest kiss he had ever had in his life! From that day on, he did his best to avoid her altogether. He had fallen hard for her but knew the rules: Saint was off-limits. Period. End of story. Yet fate was seemingly bringing them together in close proximity once again. *"Damn,"* he thought to himself.

Zion had to refocus his attention. Sharmel gave him strict orders: to make sure Saint got her loot. He had Saint's life in his hands and refused to fuck it up for either of them. With his new face and new look, Zion was ready for whatever came his way.

Zion had eyes and ears from the ATL to Mexico. He was like a Black Pablo Escobar. Although he wasn't really in "the game" anymore, he still made money. After what happened to him in The Bean, his attention was on staying alive and living for a long time. He couldn't afford to get caught up with events of the past. When he recognized a situation was even remotely similar to what he had been through, he examined it closely. If it didn't seem right to him, he moved on. Zion learned to use his past to move forward with his life, but he didn't focus on it, especially after what happened to him.

~~~~~~~~~~

"I haven't spoken to Majesti since he packed up his family and hauled ass out of The Bean," Saint whispered. She remembered how he was into all kinds of shit: robbing people, selling drugs,

and even being quick to murder. It all caught up to him. Well, better said, it caught up to his boy Quantity. They found his body in the ATL. The word on the streets was it was due to a drug deal gone wrong. Perhaps that was enough for Majesti to be convinced that he was next because whatever Quantity did, he was always there to back up his boy and vice-versa. Majesti was the type of dude who followed others but seeing that his ass could end up dead in another state slowed his roll a lot! *"Well, one thing Majesti was always good at was getting rid of the devil's product!"* Saint thought to herself.

She pulled herself together and headed back downstairs for dinner. Her mother was putting it **down** in the kitchen with that honey-glazed chicken and garlic potatoes! Mmm! The food smelled so good!

As they both sat down to eat, Saint asked her mother, *"When was the last time you spoke to Ms. Maggie?"* (Ms. Maggie is Majesti's mother and her mother's best friend.)

Ms. Handsome replied, *"Oh, Lord! Baby, it's been a while since I last talked to her."*

Ever since Ms. Maggie and her family relocated to the ATL, her mom rarely heard from her bestie. The two of them grew up together and used to do everything together. They went to bingo, attended the same church, and even dated the same guy in high school (although neither knew it at the time).

"Well, how would you like to take a mini-vacation and visit Ms. Maggie? I'm on a break from school and have some money saved," Saint subtly suggested. As she waited for her mother's response, she thought about the large sum of money she had saved for a rainy day such as the one presented.

Her mother replied, *"You know, baby, that would be a great idea! Let me give her a call. She will be so excited!"*

After dinner, Saint left her mother while she spoke with Ms. Maggie and went upstairs to her bedroom. She grabbed her Louis Vuitton purse and keys to the Range Rover, ran back downstairs, and signaled to her mother that she would be back. *"I'm going to Monae's house."* Her mother gave her a slight nod and a quick wave of her hand, indicating she had heard.

Monae and Sharmel were very tight and had been since middle school. They even attended the same high school, Jeremiah E. Burke, in Dorchester. They were high school sweethearts at one point, but Monae couldn't deal with Sharmel's lifestyle, so they split.

As Saint pulled up to Monae's house, she heard screaming from inside. *"Oh, Lord. I'm not staying here long!"* Saint said to herself. Monae was Saint's best friend and the only female friend she really had. There were so many females that hated on her, all because of the lifestyle her brothers created for her. Jealousy was a beast! As a result, Saint stayed away from the club scene and out of Boston's hood. It wasn't that she thought she was too good for the hood. After all, that's where she was born and raised. She just didn't have time for all the drama that came with being in the mix of the mess!

Saint parked in Monae's driveway, got out of the Range Rover, and walked up to the door. Although Monae still lived in the city, she lived in the quieter part: Hyde Park, which was located near Readville—a stone's throw from Dedham. *"I like living here because my children don't have to worry about dodging bullets like they did in the hood,"* Monae said one day. Her three children were fathered by the same man, but it was suspected that Sharmel was the father of her oldest girl named Sharmane. That child looked just like Sharmel! Saint knew they used to fool around but didn't want anyone to know. *"Guess what, Monae? **We know!**"* Saint had to laugh at the thought.

Monae's four-bedroom townhouse was obviously inspired by an African vibe. It was beautiful from front to back.

Saint loved going to Monae's house because they always caught up on everything happening in the hood. This particular trip was different, though. It was time to discuss plans to go to ATL. They sat in the living room, and Monae yelled for her kids to play outside in the backyard. She knew the two of them were going to have a serious conversation, considering Saint's brothers were sentenced to 15 years in prison a few days ago.

"Saint, how have you been? I know things have been rough for you these past few days," Monae stated with genuine concern.

"I am okay. I cry when I think about my brothers and worry about Mama, but I am strong." Saint wanted to get straight to business with Monae because she had to leave Saturday for ATL. When Monae tried to make more small talk, Saint cut her off to tell her what was going on. *"Monae, you are not going to believe this. When Sharmel was leaving the courtroom, he handed me a letter. In it, he stated he left Mama and me $500,000 and six bricks. Here is the kicker: He wants me to go to ATL to meet up with Majesti to help me get rid of the bricks and get more money!"*

Monae was shocked into silence for the first time in her life. Ms. Mouth Almighty was suddenly speechless. ***"Has he lost his damn mind?!"*** she screamed. *"That is why I left Sharmel.*

I wasn't down for that shit." She paused to inhale deeply. *"Okay, so how does he expect **you** to do that without getting caught up?"*

"Well, that's why I'm here. I need your help, Monae." Saint looked at her friend with pleading eyes.

Monae replied with an attitude. *"I have three kids, Saint. I'm not going to do anything that's going to keep me away from them for 15 years."*

"Listen, Monae. You are the only one I can trust. You were with Sharmel when he was taking care of his business. I know you can help me. All I need you to do is drive the six bricks down to ATL. I will make sure you are comfortable with plenty of spending money and a nice place to stay. Come on, Monae. Please? I really need you. I'm not saying I'm about to take over "the game." I just want to get those six bricks out of my possession. That's all. I certainly don't want my Mama to come across them. I'd have a lot of explaining to do!"

"Saint, I don't even know why you're bothering with your brother's mess, but I will sleep on it and get back to you."

"Thank you, Monae. Thank you so much. I better get out of here before Mama sends the State Police to look for me." The friends stood and hugged briefly. *"Oh, while you're sleeping on it, don't think I don't know about you and Sharmel fooling around 12 years*

ago. Sleep on that, too!" Saint said with a wink. She smiled as she walked out the front door, but not before seeing her friend's blushing cheeks. She jumped into her truck and sped away.

It was Friday by the time Monae called Saint to let her know she would go along with the plan. There was only one exception: she insisted on taking Sharmane with her.

"Do you think that's a good idea, Mo?" Saint asked.

"Listen, it's going to be a good idea because if I get pulled over, I can say I am taking my daughter to visit her grandmother in ATL," Monae replied confidently.

They both laughed **hysterically**!

Chapter Three

E arly Saturday morning, Saint and her Mama were getting ready for their vacation in Austell, Georgia. *"Mama, it's 3:00. The taxi will be here in five minutes to take us to the airport."* With the distance and slow-driving taxi driver, they arrived at exactly 4:26 a.m. They had to hurry their way through security and make it to their gate on time. The flight was scheduled to leave at 5:20, with arrival at 9:45 a.m. at Hartsfield Jackson International Airport.

~~~~~~~~~~

Monae and Sharmane pulled out of their driveway at 6:00 a.m. with the six bricks in the trunk of the rental car, hidden under the spare tire. By 6:21 a.m., they were headed down 95 South on their way to ATL. Saint had given Monae $3,000 for spending money on the road and the hotel reservation once they arrived in Atlanta. Per their agreement, Monae was to call every hour on the hour to inform Saint of her whereabouts, letting Saint know the mother-daughter pair was okay.

~~~~~~~~~~

When the flight landed, Saint and her mother retrieved their luggage and made their way over to the Enterprise rental car booth. They were immediately overcome by all the southern hospitality. *"You don't get this much kindness in Boston,"* commented Saint. Her mother agreed, and they both laughed. *"Hello. My name is Saint Handsome. I have a reservation to pick up a rental."*

"I can help you with that, Ms. Handsome. May I please have your driver's license?" replied the brother standing behind the counter.

Saint practically undressed him from head to toe as she handed him her license. *"Damn! He looks good enough to eat and smells good, too! I know that smell,"* Saint thought to herself. *"Excuse me, sir. How do you pronounce your name?"*

He paused what he was doing and said, *"It's pronounced* **Dai'Sung.**"

"You have a very unique name," Saint replied with a flirty smile.

"Thank you, ma'am," came the sweet response. Dai'Sung moved around the counter to get the keys to Saint's vehicle. As he did, his scent passed her nose once again.

"I know that smell. That's Burberry Touch for Men. Hmph! It should be Touch by Saint because Lord knows I want to jump all over him right now. If I weren't with Mama, it probably would've happened!" Saint mused with a quiet giggle.

Dai'Sung was a tall, handsome man with a caramel complexion and a smile to die for. He had the neatest zigzag cornrows with a fresh line-up, looking like he just left the barber shop. His eyes were slanted. Either his mother or father had to be Chinese. His eyebrows were perfect, too. Saint had never seen a man with perfect eyebrows before. *"I think I am drinking a glass of haterade right now!"* she laughed to herself.

"Are you from out of town?" Dai'Sung asked.

"Yes, I am from Boston."

"What brings you to Atlanta?"

"My mother and I are visiting my aunt."

"There's nothing wrong with visiting family!" Dai'Sung had the biggest Kool-Aid smile on his face. He never took his eyes off Saint. He thought to himself, *"With a name like Saint and a body that was ready and down for whatever, God sent me an angel!"* He gathered some papers, placed them in an envelope, and

handed them to Saint. *"Ms. Handsome, enjoy your stay here in the ATL."*

Saint and her mother located their rental and loaded their bags into the trunk before climbing into the 2011 Expedition EL. Saint typed in the address to Ms. Maggie's house into the GPS: 589 Ovalene Lane. The system read they were 28 minutes away. *"Mama, buckle up!"*

~~~~~~~~~~~~~~~

During their call, Ms. Maggie insisted that Mama and I stay at their house. Mama wasn't too keen on sleeping in anybody else's bed except her own or in a hotel, but if I knew Majesti, he was living lavishly. He got mad loot plus whatever was left over from Quantity.

"I see you done found yourself some ATL eye candy," said Saint's Mama. They both started laughing hysterically. That was the first time in a long time they both laughed that hard.

"Mama, you know I'm just focusing on school. I don't have time for a man right now. Having a man takes time and planning. I don't have time for that. I love being solo, not having to answer to anyone, and coming and going as I please. I can't get enough of it!"

"Sweetie, there's nothing wrong with being loved. Once in a while, you need somebody to love and hold you," her Mama replied gently.

"I do have someone who gives me all the affection I need."

*"**You do?!** Who?!"* Mama asked in complete surprise.

"You, Mama! You are all I need." Saint grabbed her mother's hand, held it firmly, and smiled. *"I love you, Mama."*

As they approached the residence, Saint questioned the GPS' directions. *"This is it? This **can't** be right."* Just then, the GPS voice confirmed: *"You have reached your destination."*

"Oh, Lord! Maggie done hit the lottery!" Saint's mother exclaimed excitedly. Little did she know it was **not** the lottery…

As Saint pulled into the winding driveway, Ms. Maggie and Majesti were there to greet them. Saint's mother practically jumped out of the truck while it was still moving.

*"**Maggie!**"* Saint's mother yelled out.

*"**Joyce!**"* Maggie screamed with joy. They hugged each other as if they were two sisters separated at birth. *"Oh, my God! You haven't changed a bit!"*

"*Girl, we still look good!*" Joyce replied.

"*Let's get you ladies inside and settled. I have food on the grill,*" Maggie said.

Just then, Saint's cell rang. It was Monae. "*Hey, where are you now?*"

"*We are about eight hours away,*" replied Monae.

"*That's good. We just arrived ourselves. What time do you think you will get in?*"

"*We should be pulling in no later than 11:00 p.m. We are going straight to the hotel.*"

"*Cool. I will be up. Keep in touch. Girl, Ms. Maggie done went and started the grill and invited some of her church friends over. There's no telling how long they'll be here.*"

"*Enjoy yourselves. I'll call again soon. I have to go,*" said Monae.

"*I love you, Monae. Stay safe.*"

"*Yeah, yeah, yeah,*" replied Monae before disconnecting the call.

~~~~~~~~~~

Monae thought to herself, *"That's just what Sharmel would tell me when I used to make runs for him."* They would always make passionate love the day before she was to leave and fall asleep in each other's arms, never knowing if that would be the last time they would see each other.

She recalled the last moment when Sharmel asked her to make another run for him. He wanted her to go to Chi-town, and she told him she couldn't do it anymore. Sharmel couldn't understand why not — and he didn't take kindly to people telling him no. After Monae's firm *"NO!"*, that was the end of their relationship because she wanted out of "the game." She knew the risks and wanted to change her lifestyle. Although deep inside, she truly loved Sharmel, she was unwilling to risk her life for him any longer. She wanted him to stop, too, but he was so damn selfish!

Monae and Saint always remained friends, though. She never told Saint that she was pregnant with her brother's baby. Thankfully, she was four months pregnant when she met Romey. She carried the baby in her womb so small, he didn't even know she was pregnant when they met. Until this day, he believes Sharmane is his baby girl.

[40]

Monae prayed frequently during the last eight hours of her journey. One prayer that she silently prayed was:

Dear God,

I know I'm wrong for coming to You and asking You to see me through this journey, but if You see me through, I will tell my deepest secret to Sharmel and his family: Sharmane is his little girl.

In Your Name, I pray. Amen.

It was exactly 11:30 p.m. when Monae pulled into the Courtyard Marriot Hotel's parking lot. She drove just over 16 hours straight, stopping only three times to gas up and get food for Sharmane and her. She was exhausted. All she wanted to do was get checked in and go to bed. *"Hello. I have a reservation. My name is Monae Major."* She handed the woman at the front desk her driver's license while trying to hold up just-as-tired Sharmane.

"Alright, Ms. Major. You're all set. Here are your keys. You have been set up in the penthouse. Please take the private elevator to the 15th floor. Once you get off, take a left. Your room is 1515," the woman instructed. There was a twinge of jealousy in her voice.

"Thank you," Monae replied with an attitude as she snatched the keys. She rolled her eyes at the lady. Monae knew she was being eyed down because she was an out-of-towner who just got set up in a penthouse. Monae told Sharmane to wait in the lobby while she retrieved their bags. A bellboy followed her to the truck with a luggage cart. He retrieved their bags and put them on the cart. She retrieved the bricks and held onto them. Once loaded up and ready, she handed the valet her key and quickly returned to her daughter's side. They took the elevator to the penthouse, where Monae immediately dismissed the bellboy after passing him a $50 bill.

By the time Monae turned around, Sharmane was already knocked out on the sofa in the massive living space, so she went to the fully-stocked bar and got a drink. Her eyes were drawn to a new bottle of Moet. *"Now we're talking!"* she whispered. She poured herself a glass, sat in the chair by the floor-to-ceiling window, and looked out over all of ATL, remembering the last time she was there with Sharmel.

Monae grabbed her phone to call Saint. *"Hey, Saint. We made it. We are at the Marriot in downtown Atlanta. Thank you so much, girl. This penthouse is off the chain!"*

"You're welcome, Monae. You deserve it. I mean, you put your life on the line for me, and I owe you big time. I will do anything for you and yours. You know that. Now that you are here, it's going to be about business — but we have to make it a fun ass vacation, too! Get some sleep. I will see you tomorrow."

~~~~~~~~~~

Back at Majesti's house, Ms. Maggie and Joyce were doing a lot of catching up. There was so much talking and laughing going on, Saint couldn't get her mother's attention to save her life. She chose to let them have their fun and went to sit with Majesti near the pool.

"It's really fucked up about your brothers, Saint. If you ask me, someone snitched them out," he said.

"Well, I'm not out for any kind of revenge. I'm just trying to get rid of these bricks. I know each is worth $30,000. Sharmel already schooled me on that. Of course, I'm giving you a brick for your time and service. That's yours to do what you would like. I'm not trying to be greedy because greed will get me caught up. So, I need to know your every move, Majesti: who you're working with, who you're talking to, the whole nine."

"Damn, girl! You sound just like your brother!" They laughed again and sipped their rum punch. *"Wait. **Please** don't tell me you flew with the bricks."*

"Hell no! Are you crazy?" Saint thought to herself, *"I'm not that stupid!"* She took the time to explain. *"The bricks are already here. I had someone drive them down. We will see them in the morning."*

"Wow. I definitely know you are a Handsome!" Majesti said with a laugh. "*Listen, Saint. Thanks for the brick, but I'm straight. I don't roll like that anymore. I'm comfortable right now. Sharmel is my man, and I have a lot of respect for him. He asked me to do him a favor, and I'm going to follow through with no questions asked or other expectations of a return. He looked out for me. He told me Quantity would get me caught up or killed, and while I did get caught up, he got himself killed. That's when I knew it was time for me to get out of "the game" – and out of Boston. See, Quanity was insane. He wasn't playing with a full deck. He was my boy, and I cared deeply for him, but he did some grimy shit that would have gotten us both killed. He didn't listen to anybody. In his eyes, everybody was below him – bitches, niggas, everybody. He wouldn't even listen to his own grandmother. She tried and tried to be there for him, but dude just kept fucking up. He stressed her out so bad, she had a stroke and ended up in a nursing home."*

"Wow. This shit goes deep," Saint muttered as she took another sip of punch. *"Did he have any other family?"*

Majesti took another sip of punch and laid back in the lawn chair. *"Quanity and his mother didn't get along. She was on drugs and working the streets, so he really had no words for her. She gave him to his grandmother when he was only three months old. The only time he dealt with her was when he served her."* Saint reacted in disbelief because she couldn't believe that nigga sold drugs to his own mother! Majesti continued. *"His father has been in jail since the early '80s. His sister went down the same road as his mom until some John picked her up off the street one day, put her in rehab, and married her."*

"What kind of shit is that, Majesti? Well, he must have been an angel."

"On the real, girl!" Majesti got all excited when he said that, as if he wished it was him instead of Quanity's sister. *"Dude is White. He moved her to Houston, Texas. That cat has it made out there!"* He fell silent for a moment, deep in thought. *"Quanity hooked up with this chick at one point. Her father was the head nigga in charge in the ATL. Shorty was like 17 years old when they hooked up. She was really pretty but so damn naïve! He did her*

wrong and treated her like shit, but he also kept her fly. I still don't see how she stayed with that nigga."

"What happened to her? You said 'was.'"

"She was killed. I think the people who were after Quanity killed her. She was driving his car at the time. They likely thought it was him and sprayed the car with bullets, killing her instantly. After that, I think her father ordered a hit on Quanity. I could be wrong, but that's what I heard." Saint was in shock. It sounded like a scene from a movie! *"The worst part about it was that she loved him hard."*

The two of them fell into an uncomfortable silence for a few minutes before Majesti spoke again.

"Okay. Let me take care of business. You are welcome to come along for the ride, but keep a low profile if you do. If your brother ever found out I had you with me on a mission, he would kill me! Oh! You should know the Ten Crack Commandments – or do you know them already?" asked Majesti.

"Like I said, Majesti, I'm not trying to get into "the game." I'm trying to get this shit out of my lap!"

"*I feel you, Saint,*" he replied as he rubbed his head. "*Now, drink up! You are on vacation, with your sexy ass!*" snickered Majesti.

"*Watch it now! You know I'm off-limits!*" They shared a hearty laugh and continued sipping on their rum punch.

The next morning, Saint laid in bed staring at the ceiling like she always did. That time was different, though. She had a slight hangover after drinking six glasses of rum punch. She managed to get up when she heard voices coming from the patio of the guest room. She looked out the window and saw her mother, Ms. Maggie, Majesti, his little brother Mitchell, and a young lady having breakfast. The young lady was very pretty. She must have been one of Mitchell's little friends. After all, she was a bit too young for Majesti…but then again, who knows?

Saint put on her housecoat and joined the group on the patio. "*Good morning, everyone!*"

"*Good morning,*" came the response in unison.

"*Look at you, Mitchell! So grown up!*" Saint said with a smile.

Mitchell smiled back. *"Saint, this is my girlfriend, Neveah."*

"Hello, Neveah." She then returned her attention to Mitchell. *"How have you been?"*

"I just finished my freshman year of college," he replied.

"What college do you attend?"

"I am going to Fisk University. It's an all-Black college."

"That's really good! How old are you now?" Saint asked.

"I'm 19."

"Wow! Time sure does fly by!"

After breakfast, everyone except Saint went back inside. She remained outdoors, enjoying the fresh morning air. About 30 minutes later, she went to get dressed because Majesti was waiting for her to head over to the Marriot.

~~~~~~~~~~

Around noon, Majesti and Saint were ready to meet up with Monae at the Marriot. Saint was rocking her Baby Phat skinny tuxedo jeans with a hot pink Baby Phat tee and hot pink Baby Phat Milan cat highs. Yes, she was on vacation, but she had to dress for the occasion. She didn't have anyone to get fly for — or maybe she did, as thoughts about how good Dai'Sung looked flashed through her mind. If she ever saw him again, she knew it would be on and poppin'! She made a mental note to hit the club later that night. Satisfied with her gear and appearance, she smiled at herself in the mirror and then headed downstairs.

Majesti met Saint at his 2011 Lincoln Navigator. *"Whoa! This is **hot**! Fully-loaded! Damnnnnnn!"* she exclaimed.

"Can't get no better than this! This is a grown man's truck!" Majesti replied. He was right. No flashy rims, no booming system, nothing extreme whatsoever. It was just right.

"I guess some people do grow up!" They shared a laugh.

Saint jumped into her rental and followed Majesti to the Marriot. As they approached the penthouse, they heard loud music coming from the other side of the door. Saint rang the bell, banged on the door, and even kicked the door — hard. No answer. Saint and Majesti looked at each other in dismay. Saint reached into her Coach bag, pulled out her cell, and dialed Monae's number. After six rings, Monae finally answered. *"Hello, Monae. Can you please open the door? I've been out here ringing and knocking for a while now! This is embarrassing. Thank goodness you are on your own floor!"*

Monae hung up and opened the door. When she saw Majesti, she roughly shoved Saint to the side and gave him the biggest hug ever. *"Damm! Look who the cat dragged in!"* she said with a laugh.

As they walked into the penthouse, Sharmane was just finishing her lunch. She ran up to Saint. *"Auntie!"* she screamed. She embraced Saint tightly, not wanting to let go.

"Hey, sweetie! How was your trip?"

"It was good. Long and fun. We ate a lot of junk food!"

Saint hugged her niece again and laughed.

"Well, who is this adorable little girl?" Majesti asked.

"This is my daughter Sharmane," Monae answered. The look on Majesti's face changed **instantly**. She looked just like Sharmel. The adults in the room looked back and forth at each other and shook their heads.

"*Sharmane, go and gather your things,*" Monae instructed. After leaving the room, Monae said to Majesti, "*Don't even go there.*"

"*Okay. Let's talk business,*" he replied. "*I already made some calls last night. I will be making my first drop at the club tonight. So, why don't you ladies do what you do best?*"

"*What would that be?*" asked Saint in a sarcastic tone.

"***Shop!***" he replied. "*I will meet you ladies back at my house. Monae, I would love for you and little Sharmel…I mean **Sharmane** to come to stay at the house with us.*" Monae gave him a look that could kill. "*It makes no sense paying for another night up here. Come over and hang out with the family. Plus, Sharmane could hang out with Mama and Ms. Joyce. I can invite my girl's daughter over to keep her company.*"

Monae agreed to the arrangement and packed up all their belongings. "*Sharmane, I am going to the mall with Saint. I will see you when I get back, okay? Behave and have fun!*"

Sharmane was happy to leave the hotel to play with another little girl. "*Bye, mommy!*" She grabbed her bags and walked out the door with Majesti.

After the duo left, Saint and Monae grabbed the remaining luggage, checked out of the hotel, and climbed into Saint's rental. It was a perfect summer day. As they pulled out of the parking lot, Saint opened the sunroof and rolled down the windows to let the fresh air blow. She then started blasting her newest favorite song, "Waterfalls" by TLC. That song was her anthem! Both ladies sang along and enjoyed the ride to the mall. As she drove, Saint thought to herself, *"It's summer, I am a single lady, and I'm in a different state. I am going to have fun tonight!"*

~~~~~~~~~~

Not long after their trip started, they pulled up to the Lenox Square Mall. They looked at each other in amazement. *"Damn! This is a mall? The biggest mall back home is the South Shore Plaza in Braintree. This is bigger than that. I just hope they have my kind of stores inside!"* Saint said. They both laughed.

They walked into the mall and were awestruck. It had all the stores they loved to shop in and then some: Banana Republic, True Religion, Bebe, BCBG, and more! The friends looked at each other with massive smiles on their faces. They were like two kids in a candy store!

Saint turned to Monae and said, *"Today is your lucky day, baby because we are going on a shopping spree! We must stay fly while we are here in ATL!"* Monae nodded her head yes, and they entered Bebe, where they were in dress heaven. Saint laid her eyes on a simple black dress but thought it would not be so simple once it got on her body. Monae found a dress, too: a purple short-sleeved dress with a hood. The two of them always had different styles, but their choice of style complemented who they were. Saint paid for their dresses, and they went off to the next store to get shoes and accessories.

They entered Nine West and tried on countless pairs of shoes. With each try-on, they walked up and down the aisle, modeling the shoes for each other. The two sales associates observed them, knowing they were not from Atlanta, when they heard the ladies talking loudly. Monae found herself a pair of sleek black peep-toe pumps. Saint found a pair of red closed-toe pumps with zippers in the front. The shoes were sure to add just the right WOW-factor to her black dress.

From there, they went to Macy's, Coach, Burberry, and Tiffany Co. They left the Lenox Square Mall with so many damn bags, anyone looking would've thought they bought everything in the mall!

Chapter Four

Majesti rented a Hummer limo for the night and reserved seats for them in VIP. They pulled up to Club 112 in downtown Atlanta in style, and the driver opened the door for them. Majesti stepped out first, looking fresh in his dark blue Sean John jeans, multicolored Sean John shirt, and fresh white Air Force Ones. To add that special touch, he wore his Rolex. Next, Majesti's girl Nikita stepped out. She wore a yellow halter romper with black sandals, and her hair was silk pressed. Monae followed with her purple hooded dress and peep-toe pumps. Her accessories included large loop silver earrings and silver bracelets. Her hair was fly, too. It was pulled back into a straight ponytail with just a peek of bangs. Saint was the last to exit in her black dress and red pumps with zippers. She was accessorized out, wearing diamond stud earrings and her diamond bracelet. She wore her wavy dreads loose. To finish her look, she had hazel contacts, black and silver eye shadow that gave her eyes a smoky look, and red lipstick.

Saint and Monae knew they were on fire in the ATL that night as they walked into the club. Not even the Atlanta Fire Department could put out their flames! The two of them had the time of their lives. They knew all the other chicks in the club couldn't even see them because those chicks didn't look as good as them and couldn't dress as well. Even Majesti's girl looked like Plain Jane in comparison. Still, she was pretty. She was light-skinned and short with a nice body and long brown hair. The thing Saint liked about her was that she was not stuck up. She was real. She was who she was and didn't have to spend money on the latest fashions to be cool and down to earth. She was in her last year of college, studying to be a mortician. That profession sounded really creepy to Saint, but she thought, *"To each their own!"* Monae, on the other hand, didn't like anybody. She had one friend, and that friend was Saint.

After tearing up the dance floor, the three ladies made their way back to the VIP section, where they spotted Majesti talking with some guy. To Saint's surprise, it was Dai'Sung — and he looked tasty! She had her mind on business that night and watched Majesti's every move. She moved in closer to see if she could get an earful of what the two men were discussing.

"Ladies! Ladies! Are we enjoying ourselves?" Majesti asked.

"You know it! This place is poppin'!" replied Monae.

Saint looked over at Monae and shook her head. Monae had already started drinking while they were getting dressed, so she was feeling pretty nice — and it wasn't even midnight yet! *"Yeah, this is a cool spot,"* Saint answered.

"Saint, I want you to meet someone," Majesti said, directing his attention to the man he was speaking with.

"No need for introductions," Saint said with a friendly smile. *"We've already met."*

Majesti stood there, puzzled.

"Yeah, dawg. I met this beautiful young thing at the airport with her lovely mother," Dai'Sung stated. *"However, I didn't meet this lovely lady,"* he said as he gently grabbed Monae's hand. Monae was all smiles and loved every minute of the attention he gave.

Saint decided to let Monae shine that night because she had other, more pressing plans.

Either Majesti had already informed Dai'Sung that Saint was off-limits, or he was just as drunk as Monae because that nigga was all over her. *"You ladies are tearing this club up tonight! Y'all got mad heads turning. Even the **ladies** are checking you two out!"* Dai'Sung complimented.

"They're not checking us out. They're hating on us!" Monae commented loudly.

*"Yeah, hating that they can't **be** us!"* Saint concurred.

"I must agree with you, Majesti. They are the hottest things in the ATL right now!" Dai'Sung said as he winked at Saint. Saint rolled her eyes and kept it moving. Dai'Sung peeped it, laughed it off, and turned his attention back to Monae. *"Excuse me, ladies. I have some business to attend to. I'll be right back."*

Saint couldn't believe that muthafucka! He tried to holla at her at the airport, even slipping her his cell, yet he was trying to kick it with her friend—right in front of her! Actually, Saint didn't really care as much as it may have appeared. She wasn't there to romance anyway. She was there on business. She snapped out of her zone and focused on Majesti and Dai'Sung at the bar.

As she continued to observe the two men, Monae bumped into her. That was a sign that Monae had enough to drink. She was not about to embarrass herself and nobody else. Saint was looking too good for that. She signaled to Majesti at the bar and then said to Monae, *"You're cut off, girlfriend. I think you've had enough to drink for the night."*

Majesti walked back over to the group in VIP. *"What's going on?"* he asked.

Saint quickly replied. *"Monae is fucked up. She's cut off for the rest of the night, and it's not even 12:00 yet!"* She so badly wanted to ask Majesti what his connection was to Dai'Sung, but she remembered what he said about poking her nose into his business, so she let it go.

"Saint, are you thirsty?" Majesti asked.

"You know how I am," she replied. Majesti signaled for the waitress to come over. *"I'll have Patron, chilled."* Just then, Saint's favorite reggae song, "Girl Ya Good" by Shabba Ranks, began to play. Saint was in a world all by herself. She got up and walked onto the dance floor near the bar. She was in a zone and feeling nice after four Malibu and pineapple drinks and a shot of Patron. It was all about her at that moment. She was winding and grinding her way all the way down to the floor, feeling the groove and dropping it like it was **hotttt**—all the while with her eyes closed!

When the song ended, and Saint finally opened her eyes, she immediately noticed the whole club had been watching her dance. She was so embarrassed! She then locked eyes with a guy who was staring at her intently with a slick smile. He winked at her, which prompted her to run straight to the ladies' room to get herself together. *"What the hell, Saint? Shit! All I needed was a pole after all that!"* she said to herself accusingly. She also couldn't take her mind off the guy that winked at her. There was something about him…

When Saint returned from the ladies' room, she found Monae sitting in their spot with Nikita. Nikita had Monae drinking a cold bottle of Poland Spring water.

"Girl, thank you. I really needed this," Monae managed to say as she slurred her words.

Nikita let out a little chuckle. *"It's okay, girl. I know how it is to have some fun. No worries. Ms. Ranks, that was quite a show you put on out there."*

"Show? What show?" Monae asked. *"I missed the show?"* Saint and Nikita busted out laughing.

"Last call for alcohol!" the DJ announced over the mic.

"Where the hell is Majesti, Nikita?" Saint inquired as she looked around.

"He stepped out. He will meet us outside. He said he had to take care of some business."

Saint felt a bit more at ease after Nikita said that and refocused her attention on Monae. *"Are you ready, Monae? Let's bounce before this crowd starts heading to the door. Nikita, can you text Majesti and let him know we'll be in the limo, please?"*

"I sure can. I'm right behind you."

Saint and Nikita worked to get Monae into the limo. In an instant, she passed out drunk in the seat. Majesti was nowhere in sight. Saint looked around for him in a panic. ***"What the fuck?"*** she thought.

"He'll be here shortly, Saint. Relax," Nikita said assuredly.

"Is this bitch reading my mother fuckin' mind?" Saint thought. She didn't like that feeling. *"I'm cool. I know he's a big boy,"* she replied. She continued to look around at the crowd gathering outside. *"So, this is the after-effect of clubbing in the ATL?"*

"*Yeah, girl. Everyone just stands around, kickin' it. It often looks like everybody is trying to get with anybody. Chicks hating on each other and whatnot. It's just craziness!*" Nikita laughed.

"*I feel you. It's the same in Boston.*" Saint noticed the same guy from inside the club was now staring at her outside. She wondered why he kept staring at her so intently.

"*Majesti is coming now,*" Nikita reported.

As he approached, he asked, "*Ladies, where is Monae?*"

"*She's tore up from the floor up,*" Saint said, pointing to the limo.

"*Okay. Let's roll. My work is done here for the night. What's good, Nikita? My place or yours?*"

"*Let's just go back to your house. Narvea is there, and I can't go a night without my baby.*"

On the return trip to Majesti's house, all three ladies passed out drunk in the limo while Majesti remained fully awake, thinking about his next move. When they finally arrived, he woke them up. He and the driver helped each one step out, hoping they wouldn't fall—especially Monae. After they entered the house safely and made their way to their respective rooms for the night, Majesti tipped the limo driver, headed inside, and went to bed.

Chapter Five

The next morning, Saint was the last one to get up. *"I guess that's an advantage of not having kids. I can sleep until noon or later if I want,"* she said to herself. She grabbed her housecoat, put on her slippers, and made her way to the kitchen. She had slept through breakfast, but it was just her luck that Ms. Maggie would be grilling again.

"Hey, sleepyhead," Saint's mother said to her as she entered the living room.

"Hey, Mama," she replied as she kissed her mother on her forehead. *"Where is everyone?"*

"They're out on the patio having a late breakfast."

"Mama, why are you in here alone?"

"I just needed some me-time, that's all."

"You're not thinking about the boys, are you?"

"I know I shouldn't be worrying about them. They're grown men, but they're also my boys. I really miss them."

"Mama, it's going to be alright," Saint said as she grabbed her mother's hand and looked at her dead in her eyes. *"Don't worry about them, Mama. **Please** don't worry."*

Saint's mother got up from the recliner, wiped the tears from her eyes, and kissed her daughter on the cheek. *"You're right, baby girl. I know everything will be alright. Go freshen up before Maggie's church friends get here."*

Saint laughed at her mother. *"Mama, be nice. Maggie is just making sure we have fun while we're here. You **are** having fun, right Mama?"*

"Yes, I am."

Saint looked at her with a look that said, *"Who are you kidding, lady?"* She laughed all the way to the patio. *"Hey, all!"* she said as she took a seat in a patio chair.

"Hi, Auntie!" Sharmane yelled from the other side of the pool. Saint waved at her excitedly.

Majesti was getting the grill all cleaned up for Ms. Maggie.

"So, when are you and your mom leaving, Saint?" Monae asked.

"Hopefully, Friday night. I want to be home in my **own** bed by Sunday at the latest."

Monae chuckled and nodded. "That's cool. I think Sharmane and I will pull out of here tomorrow evening."

"**What?!** Mo, you've only been here for three days!" The disappointment in her voice was unmistakable.

"Saint, I have other children at home who need their mommy. Plus, I miss my babies! My work here is done. It's time for us to head back north!"

"I understand, Monae. I appreciate everything you have done for me – more than you will ever know. I have an idea. Why don't you leave Sharmane here with Mama and me? I mean, it is summer vacation, she's having a great time here, and that will be one less child you have to worry about, at least for a little while."

Monae hesitated slightly before responding. "I don't know, Saint. You have too much going on down here."

Saint turned to face her best friend. *"Listen, I would **never** let anything happen to her. I promise she will be okay."*

"I don't know... Let me think about it," Monae said thoughtfully.

~~~~~~~~~~

"Well, well, well! Good morning, ladies! How are we doing? Is anybody up for a drink?" Majesti asked as he chuckled his way to the pool's edge to get his feet wet. *"I must say: You ladies were getting it in last night! Y'all had mad niggas **and** chicks blowing up my phone."*

Saint and Monae looked at each other and busted out with laughter. *"Hey! That's how we do!"* Monae replied. Almost simultaneously, both threw up the deuce sign. All three roared with laughter.

Once they calmed down, Majesti said, *"Well, it's time to get your church party on today. My mom has invited her church folks over for her annual church summer cookout."*

Monae couldn't believe it. *"Your mom has had more parties in one week than P. Diddy had in a month!"*

"*I know, right? It almost seems like every damn day!*" Saint replied.

"*Come on, y'all! Leave MaDukes alone! She loves her church and her family,*" Majesti said with a smile. "*She will do anything for them! That's her signature speech at every event.*"

Their laughter brought Ms. Joyce and Ms. Maggie out to the patio. "*I don't know what all the fuss is out here,*" said Ms. Maggie, "*but can you three lushes get yourselves together before people start arriving? The pastor is coming, and Mitchell is coming with Neveah and her Godfather.*"

"*Really? I was wondering when we were going to meet that cat,*" Majesti stated.

"*Majesti! Watch your mouth!*" Ms. Maggie gave him a scornful look.

"*I'm just saying, Ma. They have been dating for a while, and we have yet to see this cat. We've talked to him on the phone but have not met him in person.*"

"*Well, you'll be able to meet him today. Now, please finish the grill – and I need some ice. Oh! And please change those damn sheets downstairs. Don't think I didn't go downstairs this morning!"* With the hint taken, all three of them started walking back inside.

"Saint!" Majesti called out before she went back in. *"Let me holla at you for a sec. I want to keep you updated about what's going on."* Saint returned to his side. *"Last night, Dai'Sung copped one of those bricks. He really came through with his. He will be here later on today to drop off and pick up. You feel me? That's $20 grand in the bank for you. Now, times that by five. Girl, that's almost $100 grand and some change! My question to you is this: How in the hell are you going to get this money back to The Bean with you?"*

Saint walked over to the edge of the pool and stood looking down into the crystal-clear water for about a minute. *"I don't know, Majesti. I never really thought about that."*

"Well, think really damn hard and get at me." Majesti walked away, leaving Saint standing alone.

"Damn! What would Sharmel do?" Saint thought aloud. *"Think, girl. Think! What would he do?"*

~~~~~~~~~~

Around 1:30 p.m., people started showing up for the cookout. The pastor and his wife were the first, followed by the lady from next door with her twins. By 1:45, nearly half the church had arrived. *"I thought people are supposed to chill on Sundays,"* Saint thought to herself. Mitchell walked out to the patio without Neveah on his arm. *"Mitchell, how are you? Where is Neveah?"*

"She will be here later with her Godfather," he replied.

Majesti joined them. *"What's up, lil' bro? What's good with work?"*

"You know me, big bro! Work! Work! Work!"

Majesti nudged Mitchell on the side and asked, *"So, that pretty young thang of yours... Are you guys serious?"*

"What do you mean? Like marriage serious? No! We're trying to do this college thing and make something of ourselves. Marriage may come later, though. Who knows? Who's to say we'll even still be together when we finish college?" Mitchell said with a shrug.

Ms. Maggie chimed in the conversation on her way to the grill. *"That's right, baby. Things happen, and people change. Don't waste your young life on just one woman. Get your education and then worry about those women last!"*

Monae had slid in behind Saint, listening to the chatter. *"I know that's right! I tell Sharmane the same thing all the time: school first, boys later. Shit, I wish she would come to me talking about, 'Mommy, can I call my boyfriend?' I will choke the…"*

*"**Hello**, Pastor Williams!"* Saint loudly interrupted just as Monae was about to scream the word hell.

"How are you young folks doing this afternoon?" Pastor Williams asked.

"We're good. How about yourself?" Saint asked.

"With the Good Lord above the Great Heavens protecting us from the thugs, drug lords, molesters, and rapists, I can't complain!" There was a brief moment of awkward silence. *"Well, you young folks enjoy the rest of the day!"* he said before walking away.

The group busted into laughter, which drew the attention of the other attendees. At that moment, Neveah and her Godfather walked out onto the patio.

"Lord, have mercy on my soul. That's the same man from the club who was staring me down and winking at me!" Saint thought to herself. She felt his presence at Majesti's house had somehow embellished the whole patio with grace. He had everybody and

their Mama looking straight at him. The man was **beautiful**! He walked right over to Ms. Maggie with gracefulness and handed her 100 blooms of petite white roses. Everyone's mouth fell to the floor.

"Ms. Maggie, I am very pleased to finally meet you." He said it with gentle kindness as he offered her a slight bow at the waist. *"It would be my honor if you would please accept these roses."*

"Thank you so much, Zion. This is so kind of you. You didn't have to bring me flowers. Come. Meet my family." Zion followed Ms. Maggie to where everyone stood, staring and marveling at this man's very presence. *"Mr. Zion, this is everyone. Everyone, this is Mr. Zion."*

Majesti approached to shake Zion's hand. *"Nice to finally meet you, dude. We were wondering when we were going to get a chance to meet you in person."*

Zion gave off a little laugh and had a smirk on his face. Saint wasn't sure if anyone else peeped that. For some reason, Zion seemed a bit harsh toward Majesti, yet no one else seemed to notice but her.

After Zion was introduced, he seemed to blend right in with the crowd. Ms. Joyce had taken an instant liking to him. *"I guess it's because he's as tall as Sharmel. Not as good-looking, but he has a grandeur appearance just the same. He smelled so good, too. I know for sure that he's' the same guy from the club,"* Saint thought to herself. She couldn't even ask Monae to confirm because she was so tore up that night. Saint didn't want to ask Nikita because she didn't want that chick all up in her business. Mitchell and Neveah were having the time of their young lives. Saint chose to keep her cool and just observe Zion, but everywhere she went, he observed her. He refused to let her out of his sight.

"So, Saint… What do you think about Kemosabe over there? Oh, shit! He's coming this way, girl!" Monae said to Saint as she tried to fix herself up a bit. It was a little too late to be fixing hair and makeup because Zion was moving in fast. Saint wasn't worried about her looks. She took after her mom and dad. She knew she was beautiful, with or without makeup. Monae was, too, but she always needed reassurance.

"Ladies, how are we doing over here?" Zion asked Saint and Monae.

"We're doing just fine. How about yourself?" Saint asked. *"Oh, my* **GOD**! *This man is amazing! There's something about him…"* she thought.

"I'm good. I never got your names."

"Well, I'm Saint, and this is Monae."

Zion laughed as he covered his shy, beautiful smile. *"Saint and Monae."* He laughed again and then let out a sigh.

"What's so funny?" Saint asked as she giggled and looked at Monae in confusion. *"Weren't you at Club 112 in downtown Atlanta last night?"*

"Yes, I was."

"I knew it. I knew you looked familiar," Saint stated confidently. Zion and Saint started laughing as if they had known each other for years. *"I thought I recognized you. You were standing near the bar with a toothpick in your mouth."*

"Wow! How could you have seen that when you were on the dance floor with your eyes closed, putting on a show that would shame any exotic dancer? I meant that as a compliment, by the way." Saint started to blush instantly. She placed her hands over her face to cover the embarrassment.

"What happened? What did I miss?" asked Monae.

"Nothing much," Zion responded. *"Your girl here was having a lot of fun last night. That's all."* He bowed his head slightly at each of the ladies before saying, *"Well, it was nice talking to you both. Enjoy the rest of the evening."* He walked back to where Mitchell and Neveah were sitting and then strolled to the edge of the pool, standing with his hands in his pockets and legs spread wide open, staring into the water. A reflection of who he thought was Shein stared back at him. He was lost in thought until Saint came up behind him and gave him a little play push as if she was going to throw him in. Wow! The reflection was actually Saint's! *"Whoa! Whoa! Not my white linen suit!"* Zion said with a broad smile. He playfully grabbed her hand to catch his balance.

Saint began to laugh. *"I wouldn't do that to you."*

"Saint, I know this will sound strange coming from a stranger and all, but I need to talk to you about something very important."

Saint had a look on her face that said, *"What in the hell? I don't even **know** this character!"* She straightened up, looked him in the eyes, and asked, *"What do you need to talk to **me** about?"*

"Listen, I can't talk to you about it here. I will be in the ATL for a while. I'll give you my number. Please call me when you have a private moment, and I will explain everything to you. All you need to know is that Sharmel sent me here. So, trust me, okay? Just trust me. And to answer your question: Everybody is going to die someday."

One part of Saint wanted to beat the shit out of him for saying some crap like that, while the other part of her wanted to know what in the hell he wanted to talk about. How does he even know Sharmel?!

Zion walked away from Saint with a look of sorrow on his face. He wanted to tell her right then why he was there, but he couldn't do it there. He needed to have her alone so she would understand what was happening. He had no idea how she would react. She didn't even notice it was Mykal that she was talking to. It was apparent his new face and new name were working to hide his true identity, but he had to let her know the truth. He had to earn her **trust**! To him, Saint was still beautiful and pure as olive oil. The only downfall was that she was his man's sister, which kept her off-limits.

"Come on over, Saint! We're taking pictures!" Monae called out.

Saint was not in the mood to take pictures or talk to anyone at that moment. She really wanted to know what the hell that conversation with Zion was all about. What just happened? She didn't want to show her true colors, so she went ahead and joined the group to take pictures. Zion suggested that he and Saint take one together. Everyone thought it was cute. Saint thought it was bullshit. *"Hopefully, it will come out nice,"* Zion said.

"I know, right?" Saint laughed uneasily and agreed.

Majesti walked over and joined the small group of friends. *"Hello! Hello, all! So, Zion, how long have you lived in Atlanta?"*

"For about ten years now."

"What type of business are you into?" Majesti asked.

"I'm in the car business."

"Oh? You own a car dealership?"

"I own three dealerships. They were my dad's. I took them over about five years ago after he passed. I have one out here called BEME Dealers."

"Yeah, yeah, yeah! I'm familiar. It's on Peachtree Industrial Boulevard. I went there to look at some Navigators and Expeditions," Majesti said while rubbing his chin.

"Really? What did you end up getting?" Zion asked.

"I went with the Nav, straight from the top of the line."

Zion wasn't really trying to hear anything Majesti had to say. In the back of his head, he was thinking, *"This muthafucka sounds shady."* He wanted to check him right then and there but knew it was neither the place nor the time. *"Excuse me. Let me check on Neveah. Nice talking to you."* Zion looked at Saint, but she looked away, avoiding his gaze.

~~~~~~~~~~

"Majesti, when is Dai'Sung coming?" Saint asked.

"Speaking of that nigga, let me call him. He said he would be here by 4:00. It's damn well near 6:00 now." Majesti dialed up Dai'Sung on the cell.

After the first ring, he answered. *"Nigga, I'm pulling up in the driveway right now. I hope MaDukes still got the grill going. A brutha is **starving!**"*

"Yeah, she's still throwing down, but she's about to shut it down."

"Aight, nigga. I'm right here. Get off my line!" Dai'Sung walked right to the back with a briefcase. All Saint could do was smile, right along with Majesti.

Zion kept a careful, watchful eye on the trio. He knew just what was going down. The simple fact was that Dai'Sung worked for him. Dai'Sung played his position and let Majesti do this thing. After saying hello to everyone and grabbing a plate of food, he followed Majesti into the house and down to the basement.

"About time, mofo! It better all be here, nigga," Majesti said.

"It's all there, man. You know how I roll," Dai'Sung replied. *"Check this out. I think I got another hustle for you. I'm going to let him taste what I got, and if he likes it, I'll set up the meeting."*

"No doubt," said Majesti. *"Let him know I'm not taking any shorts. Either come correct or don't come at all."*

"You got that, M. I got to hit the road now. I have a long drive and don't want to get caught riding dirty. You know what I mean?"

"Yeah, dude. No doubt, no doubt. Make sure you hit me up when your boy is ready," Majesti instructed.

"I'll see myself out. Stay up, man."

Once Dai'Sung showed himself out, Majesti helped himself to his share of the loot. He took $10 grand from the $30 grand in the briefcase. His plan was to take $10,000 from each $30,000 brick that he sold. He had already informed Saint that they were not going to sell them for $30 grand. The most she would get for each brick would be $20 grand.

By the time Majesti made it back upstairs, everybody was almost gone. Monae was upstairs, packing for the return trip home. She was leaving in the morning and had decided to take Sharmane home with her. It was cool with Saint because she was going to be a bit tied up anyway.

~~~~~~~~~~

Before leaving the cookout, Zion and Neveah came over to say goodbye. *"Listen. Let me know when you get that picture developed."*

"I will," Saint replied with a roll of her eyes. *"I will do it before I leave. I'll be here a few more days. Have a safe drive home."*

"Ms. Maggie, thank you for your hospitality. Next time, let's do this at my place," Zion suggested.

"You're so very welcome. Anytime, baby. Anytime. I packed a basket to take with you. There's plenty for tomorrow, too," Ms. Maggie said as she handed them a literal picnic basket packed with food.

"Oh, Ms. Maggie! You didn't have to do that!" Zion said shyly.

"I know, but I did. Now, take it and get that baby home."

"Okay. Okay. If you insist," Zion replied. *"Thanks again!"*

On the two-hour drive home, Neveah slept silently. Zion was still amazed and overtaken by Saint's beauty and kindness. The way she spoke was so elegant, and the way she walked took his breath away. He reminisced about when she playfully acted like she was going to push him into the pool. Honestly, her touch made his penis rise—something he hadn't felt in a long time. *"Damnit! What am I thinking?"* he asked himself. *"I'm here to do a job. That's it."*

Just as he was coming out of his paradise, his cell rang. It was Dai'Sung. *"Yo, what's the deal?"* Zion asked.

"Yo, man. You were so right. That dude is shady. He told Saint that no one would buy those bricks at the cost Sharmel told her. He plans to take a $10,000 cut from each brick that sells. I am setting him up with another hustle," Dai'Sung reported.

"That's cool. Pick up the money tomorrow. I will meet you at the spot. This time, I want you to set him up with Nazen. I want Nazen to shake him up a little bit. Call me as soon as Nazen's done. He's probably going to call me first. Peace out." Zion thought to himself, "Is that cat for real? Just because Sharmel is locked up, he really thinks he can fuck him over and play his little sister like that?"

Zion was so furious that he took a long, steaming hot shower and went straight to bed.

Chapter Six

The next morning, Monae and Sharmane were all packed up and ready to go. Ms. Maggie had made them a wonderful breakfast and a basket of leftovers to take on the plane. Monae looked sad as she watched Majesti load up their luggage. *"Listen, Saint. We had so much fun and enjoyed our mini vacation. It's time for us to get back home to our family."*

Saint needed to see a smile on her bestie's face. After all, she had risked so much. *"I will see you when I get back. Let's plan a shopping trip and a night out so that we can party like rock stars again!"* She was overjoyed to see a smile return to her friend's face.

Majesti and Saint drove Monae and Sharmane to the airport. Once the luggage was unloaded, the group hugged and gave each other kisses goodbye. *"Have a safe flight, you two. I will see you when I get back!"* In the blink of an eye, the mother-daughter team disappeared into the crowd of travelers.

As Majesti expertly navigated his way out of the airport, he suggested they go have a bite to eat. *"Sounds good to me,"* Saint agreed.

"What do you feel like eating?" Majesti asked.

"Umm… I don't know. Something light. Do you guys have Panera Bread down here? I could go for a Chicken Caesar sandwich with a large green tea."

"We do! Panera Bread it is!" Majestic was pleased to give the beautiful Saint her heart's desire.

Once they arrived, they took a seat in the cozy atmosphere. The young waitress handed each of them a menu, which Saint handed right back. "I don't need this. I already know what I want. I'll have a Chicken Caesar sandwich and a large green tea." Saint was impressed that the waitress didn't even have a notepad in hand. She was obviously committing their order to memory.

"And how about you, sir?"

"I will have the same, but change the drink to a large Pepsi, please," Majesti replied. The waitress nodded and walked away. "So, per our last conversation, you were going to try and figure out how you would get the money back home. Have you given it any thought?"

Saint's hesitation in response was long enough to have their food and drinks served. When the waitress walked away again, she finally said, *"No, Majesti. I have not given it any thought. It's not like I can call Sharmel and ask him to figure it out for me. That's why he sent me to you! You used to work for him. Y'all did this kind of stuff all the time."*

"Whoa! Slow down, lil' lady! I just wanted to know if you had given it any thought. That's all. I honestly don't think you and your mom should fly back home. For one, you would have a lot of explaining to do when the briefcase goes through the x-ray machine and they see all that money. For two, your mom will kill you if you get busted."

*"Well, what should I do then, Mr. Rich Man? **What?**"* Saint was practically yelling, which drew the attention of everyone in the restaurant.

Majesti placed his hand on hers. *"Damn, Saint. I know you're stressed out, but chill for a minute."*

"Sorry, Majesti. I just want to be done with this shit!" She was on the verge of bursting into tears but sucked it all back in.

"Look at me, Saint. This is the plan. I hope to have it all gone by Friday, no later than Saturday. You must try to convince your mother to drive back or take the train. It's going to take a day or two

to get back home, but that's the only way you'll get the loot home without getting caught up. I have another hustle going down soon. I haven't made a move because homeboy is only willing to do less than you and I had previously discussed. Are you cool with that?"

"Yes! Yes, Majesti. Whatever it takes. As long as this business is done and my Mama and I can get out of here, I'm good with **whatever** at this point."

~~~~~~~~~~

On Tuesday, Saint was in the den watching TV with her mother and Ms. Maggie. *"So, Mama, I was thinking we could take the train back home or rent a car and drive back. I want to show you the scenic route of all the states from here to home."*

*"**Saint, have you lost your mind?!** Child, it will take us two days to get home if we do that! Plus, I ain't the one for sitting for a long time."*

"Aww! Come on, Mama. It would be fun!"

"Hmph! If you want to take a train, go right ahead, girl. I ain't taking no train when it only takes us a few hours to get home by plane. Plus, I have a doctor's appointment on Monday. I want to be well-rested, and I wouldn't be if I didn't fly home."

"I know that's right," chimed in Ms. Maggie.

Saint knew she was screwed. When her mother made up her mind, she stayed with it!

~~~~~~~~~~

Majesti was on his way to meet up with Dai'Sung and his hustle. They were meeting at Dai'Sung's crib, which was on the borderline of Georgia and Florida. *"This nigga better come correct,"* Majesti thought. *"I ain't got no time for games."*

When he was close, he got a call from Dai'Sung. *"You almost here, nigga? This dude don't wanna wait."*

"GPS says I'm five minutes away, nigga. Entertain that muthafucka until I get there!" Majesti was immediately irritated and disconnected the call quickly. *"If my boy Quanity were here, we would have robbed both those suckas!"* When he finally pulled up to Dai'Sung's crib, he was greeted by two very aggressive, stocky, red-nosed Pitbulls. Majesti called Dai'Sung. **"Man, come get these damn animals! They won't even let me open my damn car door!"** he demanded.

Dai'Sung called the dogs and put them in their cages. *"Damn, dawg. My bad,"* he said apologetically as they walked into the house. Dai'Sung lived with his mother and little sister. His father passed away a long time ago. Majesti followed him onto the patio, where his homeboy was waiting.

"The crib is looking hot, D!" Majestic complimented.

"I try, nigga. Thanks to MaDukes, though. She's dating some bigwig who owns a landscaping company."

"For real? Yo, hook a brotha up!"

Dai'Sung gave him a fist bump. *"No doubt, my nigga. I got you."* He then turned to his homeboy. *"Nazen, this is Majesti."*

"What's good?" Majesti greeted with a nod.

"I'll be right back, dudes. Y'all handle your business," Dai'Sung said.

"So, what you got for me?" Nazen asked.

"I don't ride dirty, but I did bring you a little sample," Majesti replied.

"That's cool. Let's see what you got."

Majesti laid out what he had on the table. Nazen took his fingertip, dabbed it in the white powder, and then laid it on his wet tongue.

Dai'Sung returned with three beers in hand.

"I'm straight, D. I only came to do business, not socialize," Majesti stated irritably.

"Damn, nigga! It's just a beer!"

"I'm just saying. I like to have a clear head when I'm doing business."

"Aight, aight. I feel you on that." Dai'Sung set the beers on the opposite side of the table. *"It's there whenever you want it."*

"This is some good shit you got here, son. I will definitely see you again," Nazen stated.

"Naw, dawg. You won't see me again. I'm doing someone a favor. I don't run the game like that anymore," Majesti responded.

Nazen looked at Majesti suspiciously. *"Yo, man. I thought that once you're in the game, there are only two ways out: murder or confinement."*

Majesti chuckled at this cat. *"Listen. I'm sorry. What's your name again?"*

"Nazen."

"Well, Nazen, I don't work for no one. I'm my own boss."

Nazen laughed. *"I feel you on that, dawg. We cool. So, when should I pick up? I'm ready to do the drop-off."*

"I can meet up with you tomorrow back here – if that's okay with you, Dai'Sung." Majesti waited for what he felt was a millisecond too long for his boy's reply.

"Nigga, that's cool with me. Now drink the damn beer and loosen your damn panties!"

The three men stood around and chatted about nonsense while drinking their beers. When they were done, Nazen was the first to leave. *"Aight, D. I'm out of here."*

"Aight, Nazen. Stay up."

"Will do. See y'all tomorrow at 2:00 p.m." They fist-bumped each other, and Nazen departed.

Once Nazen's car was out of sight, Majesti said, *"Yo, I'm out of here, too. I have a long ride back. Plus, I gotta check on my girl."*

"Aight, dawg. One." Another fist bump, and Majesti was gone.

On the ride home, Majesti was amped to the point of no return. He punched the steering wheel and yelled, ***"Who in the fuck did that muthafucka think he was, talking to me that way with his disrespectful ass?"*** He quieted down and thought about all the crazy shit he and Quanity had done back in the day. Back then, he wouldn't have let any shit slide, and neither would have Quanity. The dude would have been shut down on the spot and left for dead. Majesti was so heated, he didn't even realize he had arrived home. He went straight to his room because he didn't want to talk to anyone until he cleared his head about what had just gone down.

~~~~~~~~~~

The next morning, Saint was up early. She was thinking about what Zion had said to her about trusting him and that Sharmel had sent him. She was really confused. She was also trying to figure out what he meant when he said, *"Everybody will die someday."* What in the hell was **that** supposed to mean?

She decided to give him a call so that they could meet up. She hesitantly called the number Zion gave her. Just as she was about to hang up, she heard a man's voice on the other end.

"*Speak,*" he said.

Who in the hell answers the phone like that? She didn't respond.

"*Saint, is this you?*" Zion asked. *'Thanks for calling me.*"

Saint thought to herself, "*What in the hell? Is this guy psychic? How does he know it's me?*"

What she didn't know was that Zion had a cell for everything: business, the ladies, his workers...and now, one just for her.

Saint finally found her voice. "*Listen, I'm not sure who you are, what you want, and how you know my brother. But on the real, I don't have time for funny business.*"

"*Saint, listen to me. I need you to come to my house. I will send a car for you, or you can catch a cab.*"

"*I really don't need your services. I have a car.*"

"Okay. That's good. I will text you my address. Please trust me on this, Saint. Don't tell anyone about where you're going, not even your mom. I promise: You will understand when you get here. Please trust me."

Saint was on the other end of the call thinking, *"This dude is really serious!"* She said to him, "Okay. Give me an hour. No funny shit or I will call the police."

"Agreed," Zion said before ending the call.

Saint wasn't stupid. Regardless of what Zion advised, she sent Monae a text message about the conversation she and Zion had, along with his address. *"If you don't hear from me in two hours, call my mom."* She then hit the send button.

Saint showered, dried off, and got dressed. Her gear of choice was her Akademiks one-piece blue jean short set and rhinestone strappy heels. She shined up her body with Lavender body oil and let her dreads flow. She knew she was looking good. She thought, *"Shit, if I'm gonna go out, I'm gonna do it looking damn good!"* Before grabbing her keys, she finished her look with baby pink lip gloss by Maybelline. She called out to her mother, *"I'm going to the mall. I'll be back in a few hours."*

~~~~~~~~~~~

Majesti was up early as well and had a down-for-whatever attitude. He left the house right after Saint did. He was in such a rush, he didn't say a word to anyone, not even his mom. He always told her where he was going and what time to expect him back, but today was different.

He decided he wasn't even going to call Dai'Sung to let him know he was on the way. They knew what time to expect him anyway. This time, they were going to play by his rules. No more being Mister Nice Guy. Dai'Sung was cool, but he couldn't be trusted.

Majesti sat in Dai'Sung's driveway for about 20 minutes, thinking about how he was going to handle Nazen. *"I swear: If this cat comes out of his mouth the wrong way like he did yesterday, that will be his **last** time coming at anyone like that!"* He turned off his truck, reached into the backseat to retrieve the briefcase, walked up to Dai'Sung's front door, and rang the bell.

Dai'Sung's mother answered the door. *"Hello, Majesti! How are you?"*

"Good, thank you."

"Dai'Sung is on the patio. Come in. Can I get you something to drink?"

"No, Ms. Lee. I'm fine but thank you." Majesti made his way to the patio.

"About time, nigga! What took you so long?" D asked.

Majesti let out a little chuckle as he gave D some dap. Nazen stood and gave Majesti a dap as well. Even though Majesti didn't want to accept it, he did.

"So, what do you have for me?" Nazen asked immediately.

Majesti thought to himself, *"I have a 45 to the head if you keep fucking with me!"* He replied, *"It's what do **you** have for **me**, dawg?"*

"Oh. I got you right here, Majesti. I didn't come empty-handed."

Both men exchanged briefcases.

"No need to count it. It's all there. $30 grand," Nazen said.

"That's what's up," Majesti replied with the biggest smile. In his mind, he was already laying out the plans he had for his $10,000 cut. He had told Saint he was letting this brick go for $20 grand, but he had other plans to keep his pockets fat. Once

the deal was done, he turned to D and said, *"I think I'll have that beer now."* An even bigger smile was plastered on his face.

"Yo, D," said Nazen. *"I have a long drive. I will get up with you later. Majesti, nice doing business with you. I am **sure** I will see you again. One!"* He walked off the patio, out the front door, and sped off — never looking back.

Majesti had money on his mind and his mind on his money. He didn't really pay Nazen's comment about seeing him again any attention — and he felt no guilt about lying to Saint regarding the amount of money he was selling each brick for.

~~~~~~~~~~

When Saint pulled up to Zion's house, she couldn't believe her eyes. The place was so immaculate and far better than what she and her mother lived in. The grounds were well-kept, and the garden was amazing! She sat in the car for about ten minutes, trying to reassure herself that everything would be okay. She still wondered how Zion knew Sharmel and what it was that he wanted from her. *"Why does he want me to trust him so much?"*

Saint got out of the truck and walked up to the front door. There, she was greeted by an elderly lady planting flowers. *"Ms. Saint?"* she asked.

"Yes, ma'am."

"Zion is waiting for you on the patio. Follow me."

"Thank you." As Saint followed the woman, she thought to herself, *"Damn! This muthafucka got a maid and shit! What is **really** going on?"* At that point, she was tempted to turn around, return to her car, and get out of there, but her curiosity had gotten the best of her. She chose to stay and hear him out.

When Saint reached the patio, the woman announced her arrival to Zion. *"Thank you, auntie."*

"I will bring you both some sweet tea," she said as she flashed a warm smile at Saint.

Zion took a deep breath and offered Saint a seat. Saint declined the offer and remained standing. *"Let's cut through the B.S. What do you want with me? How do you know my brother? And why in the hell should I trust you?"*

Zion walked over to Saint, grabbed her by the waist, and kissed her. Saint did not resist. There was so much passion that seemingly electrified the entire outdoors. He pulled back slightly, looked her in the eyes, and said, *"You asked me a long time ago if I was afraid to die. At the time, I didn't have an answer for you. Well, I do now. No, I am not afraid to die. I would even die for you if I had to."*

Saint pushed him away violently. She was mortified! **What in the world?!** She walked over to the edge of the Olympic-sized pool to gather her thoughts.

At that moment, Zion's aunt returned with the sweet tea on a silver platter, complete with a silver pitcher and two matching mugs.

Saint couldn't believe what she had heard. Mykal was the only person she ever asked that question to. She recalled the moment clearly because she asked him the same night she was going to give herself to him, but he declined her advances because she was Sharmel's little sister—and she was off-limits. Period. End of story.

Zion realized it was all a bit much for Saint to take in, so he decided to give her some time alone and went into the house.

Saint sat on a lawn chair near the edge of the pool and cried her eyes out. She could not wrap her head around the reality of what Zion had just said. She cried so hard and for so long, she fell asleep. About 30 minutes later, she woke up to Zion sitting across from her, staring at her intently. Saint wiped her face and asked him, *"Why am I here?"*

Zion handed her the letter Sharmel had written to him. Saint read the letter from beginning to end, handed it back, and asked, *"What does this have to do with me? And for the last time, **why am I here?"*** Before Zion could answer either question, Saint continued. *"Damn. All this time, I thought you were dead, yet all along, Sharmel knew where you were. Here you are with your new face and new life. You got it made, right Mykal? All while my brothers sit in prison, you're out here getting it in! And you want me to **trust** you? You're full of shit!"* She made no attempt to hide her rage. She grabbed her purse and keys and stormed into the house, prepared to leave.

Zion followed her. *"Listen to me, Saint. You're here because Majesti is trying to play you."*

*"What? Play me? **Me?!** Let's not stand here and talk about being played, Mykal!"*

"Are you going to listen or not?"

Saint looked at Zion and just bawled her eyes out. She had always loved him, although it was a hidden love. She had to hide her love for him from her brothers and the whole game. She knew she could trust him; she was just angry that she was left to pick up Sharmel's pieces.

Zion slowly led her back to the patio, where he gave her some tissue to clean up her face. *"Majesti is trying to play you, Saint."*

"What do you mean? Sharmel sent me to him so that he could help get some bricks off, and that's what he's doing."

"Yeah, he's doing it — but he's coming up short."

"Short? No, he's not. He's giving me mine!"

*"Oh? Really? Is he giving you what's yours, or is he giving you what he **wants** to give you?"*

"I don't understand."

"Listen. Sharmel's bricks are solid and worth every penny. How much did Majesti say he was getting for each?"

"He told me that no one would pay full price nowadays and that the most I would get per brick would be $20 grand."

Zion stood and banged on the table. ***"Majesti is straight-up lying!"***

"And how would you know?"

"I know because I'm the one who has been making the buys. I already bought two bricks from that muthafucka at $30 grand a pop. Saint, he's been pocketing $10 grand on each brick."

Saint was blown away. *"I don't understand. Why would he do that when I offered him his own brick at no charge?"*

"I hate to be the one to tell you this, but that's how "the game" works."

Saint wanted to cry. It does not feel good to be played. Anger began to fill her very soul. *"Okay. So, what do I do now?"*

*"**You** are not going to do **anything**."*

"And how am I supposed to get all that money back to The Bean?"

Zion sat back down and said, *"This is what you are going to do. I want you to give me the money."* Saint looked at him like he had six heads. *"Listen, you can't take it on the plane."*

"I know. I know." She was truly beyond frustrated.

"You're going to tell Majesti that you and your mom are leaving on Friday. Tell him Monae flew in this morning to get the money and then drove it back and that you want him to handle business while you're gone. Lastly, tell him you'll be back on Friday for the rest. In the meantime, I will be setting up three more meetings. I want you to…"

"Hold on. My cell is ringing." She looked at the caller ID and saw it was Monae calling. *"Hey, girl! Yes. Uh-huh. Okay. I will call you back in an hour. Stay by the phone."* She hung up and returned her attention to Zion.

"As I was saying, I want you to call Monae and tell her to visit Sharmel. Tell her everything I just told you about Majesti and that you need her to relay the message to your brother." Saint was listening closely. *"Saint, trust me when I say that Majesti has played his last card. I'm sorry about everything. I wish you could find it in your heart to forgive me,"* Zion pleaded. He planted a gentle kiss on her forehead and then walked her to her truck. *"Please keep*

everything between you and Monae. No one is to know about me. I still have unfinished business out there."

~~~~~~~~~~

By the time Saint arrived back at Majesti's house, everyone was having dinner. *"Saint, baby, I saved you a plate."*

"Thanks, Ms. Maggie, but I ate at the mall with Monae."

"Monae was in town?" Majesti asked, surprised.

"Yeah. She flew in this morning. She was just passing through on the way to visit her aunt in Alabama."

"Did she have the kids with her?"

"No. She was by herself. She planned on flying back home with her aunt, but she's scared to fly, so Monae is going to drive back."

"I bought a present for you. It's in your closet. I hope you like it," Majesti said with a wink.

"Thanks." Saint was grinding her teeth all the way up the stairs. ***"How dare him!"*** she thought. She had to keep her cool because she couldn't blow Zion's cover. She walked over to the closet, opened the doors, and immediately noticed two briefcases. She shut the doors and then went into the bathroom

to run a bubble bath. While she waited for the tub to fill, her phone rang. It was Monae. *"Hello?"*

"Hey, girl! Are you okay? You said you were going to call me in two hours."

"Girl, I have so much to tell you. You're not going to believe a word. Give me a bit, though. I promise I will call back after I take my bath." After her bath, she called Monae and told her about everything that had transpired that day. As expected, Monae couldn't believe the part about Mykal being Zion and, worse yet, how Majesti was playing her.

"Damn, Saint! That is crazy! Sharmel is not going to like this news at all. I'll go and tell him for you, though."

"Please and thank you. Oh! And let him know Mama and I will be home Saturday afternoon."

"Okay. I will. Saint, girl, get some rest. I will call you tomorrow night. Give Zion a kiss for me, okay?" she said with a laugh.

"Whatever, Monae! Good night." As soon as the call ended, Saint sent Zion a text:

"I will bring you the money tomorrow when Majesti leaves the house. I already told everyone that Monae was in town, which was why I was gone so long. Majesti gave me another briefcase, so that makes two. I'm going to tell him that Monae will be driving the loot back to The Bean."

Not even ten seconds later, she received a reply:

"Good job, babe. See you in the morning. Kisses!"

Saint blushed, tuned the radio to the nightly slow jams, and fell fast asleep with a smile on her face.

~~~~~~~~~~

After Monae hung up from the call with Saint, she called MCI-Cedar Junction Correctional Facility to get the visiting hours for Sharmel. She was in luck! They had visitation tomorrow! Not only was it visiting day for Sharmel, but it was a contact visit at that.

The next day, she dropped her kids off at her mother's and hauled ass to the facility. She hit 93 South and kept it moving. When she arrived, she realized it was possible Sharmel might already have another chick visiting him. Monae sucked her teeth, rolled her eyes, and removed all her jewelry before going inside. She was just another Plain Jane walking up in there. *"Damn! This line is long!"* she thought to herself. She scanned the room. There were only elderly ladies and chicks with their kids. Sharmel had one child — Sharmane — and she wasn't there. There was one chick sitting against the wall alone. *"Hmm... She could be here for him, but if she is, that's too damn bad because we will be splitting this visit!"*

Just then, the security guard called Monae's name. Instantly, butterflies filled the pit of her stomach. She stood and walked over to the guard. *"This way, please,"* he said. He led her to the visiting room and instructed her to have a seat.

Monae was a nervous wreck. She started playing with her fingers nervously, thinking about what she would say to Sharmel first. She wanted so badly to tell him Sharmane was his child, but she didn't know how he would react. She decided to start by giving him a passionate kiss. He loved the way she kissed him — something he told her all the time.

Sharmel finally walked into the visiting room. Before Monae knew it, he had wrapped her in his arm and gave her a kiss that almost made her drop her panties and throw them across the room. She didn't want to let him go. They kept at it until the guard called out, **"Handsome!"** Sharmel pulled away, licked his lips, and took a seat. Monae was speechless. No matter how often they argued or disagreed, she was still the love of his life, and he was hers.

"So, what brings you up here?" Sharmel asked.

"You look good, Sharmel."

"You look damn good, too!"

"What's good? Why are you here? Is everything okay with my mom and sis?"

"They're fine. They're still in the ATL, doing it up," Monae reported. She knew she didn't have much time, so she had to hurry — just in case some stupid ass chick came up in here and split her visit in half. *"Listen, Sharmel. I came up here for two things. First thing's first. Majesti is..."*

That's all Monae had to say. Sharmel stood, started to rub his head, and then walked over to the window under the guard's watchful eye. She could tell he was already frustrated.

"Sharmel, come here and sit down, please. I need you to listen." He slowly made his way back to his seat. *"Majesti is already starting to act shady."*

Sharmel banged his fist on the table. The guard again called out, ***"Handsome! Give it a rest!"***

"Okay. Tell me what's up. What is Majesti doing? Is he giving her money?"

"Yes. She said that he told her no one was willing to pay your asking price for the brownstones, so he is letting them go at a discount."

"Nah, man. That's bull. Those houses have been in the family for years. No discounts! Taking anything less than what they're worth is outright thievery!" He shook his head angrily. *"You've got to be kidding me, right?"*

"No one is kidding, Sharmel. Majesti is on some B.S. right now. Saint doesn't even know how she is supposed to get the money back home without getting caught up. She is a mess, Sharmel."

Sharmel continued staring at the table in silence. Monae was waiting for him to say something...anything. *"Listen to me and listen to me good, Monae."* Sharmel took Monae's hand and looked into her eye. She knew whenever Sharmel did that, things were serious, and that meant business was going to get handled—one way or another. *"Majesti is trying to pull something over on me. Because I'm in here, he thinks he can't be* *touched. **He knows the rules!***" Sharmel said as he banged on the table again and raised his voice. That caught the guard's attention, but he remained silent that time.

Monae grabbed Sharmel's hand, released it, and then placed his face in between both of her hands. Sharmel was in tears. He snatched his face away, but she grabbed it again. "*Baby, I will fix this. Tell me what to do,*" Monae said quietly.

Sharmel inhaled deeply before speaking. "*I need you to keep what I'm about to tell you to yourself, Monae. No one – and I mean no one – is to know what I'm about to tell you. It has to be like the old days. Just me and you. Do you understand me? I trust you, Monae. I always have.*" Monae nodded yes. "*I need for you to contact my boy Zion. He's from Miami.*"

"*Wait, Sharmel. That's the second thing I needed to tell you. Zion has already told Saint who he is. He's the one who told her what Majesti is up to.*"

Sharmel leaned back thoughtfully. "*Zion is five steps ahead of Majesti. I knew something like this would happen, which is why we were ahead of the game at all times.*"

"***Five minutes!***" the guard yelled.

"*Mo, listen. Things are about to get really ugly out there. There's nothing I can do because I'm in here. Make sure you get my mom and sister back home safely. Leave the rest to Zion.*" Sharmel kissed Monae goodbye, looked her in the eyes, and said, "*Like old times, baby. Me and you,*" and walked away.

Monae walked out of the prison with tears in her eyes. They were tears of love for Sharmel. Right then and there, she realized how much she loved him, how much she cared, and how much she really needed him. Once in her car, she let the tears fall freely. She cried out so loud, the chick parked next to her was looking at her strangely. Monae banged the steering wheel with her fists and asked herself time and again, **"Why is this happening? Why?"** She eventually got herself together, buckled her seatbelt, and sped off. She drove like a bat out of hell the entire way home, eager to arrive, take a hot bath, relax, and clear her head.

Chapter Seven

I t's been five years since Shein's death. Those were the words Unique repeated in her head. If only she had remained faithful to him and her crew, he wouldn't be gone, and she wouldn't be in rehab recovering from her nightmare of drugs and prostitution. The worst part of the ordeal for her was learning she was HIV positive—something she had to live with for the rest of her life. *"This is my payback, I suppose,"* she thought to herself.

Nurse "Tennessee" Jones called out to Unique. *"It's time for your meds."* Unique walked over to the window to get her meds—the ones to extend her life that she would be taking until her dying day. There was no cure for HIV. It could only be managed with medications.

Unique used to be a prostitute with a drug addiction. She had been in rehab for two-and-a-half years. No one knew where she was. She ended up there after Ricardo left her for dead in a crackhouse, where she had overdosed on Heroin. If it weren't for an old friend of her mom's, she would have died that day. "Tennessee" is what they called her because some pimp had brought her in from Tennessee in the early '80s to put in work. In no time at all, she gained mad respect from the other streetwalkers. That same woman used to run with Unique's mother back in the day. Nurse Jones was the one who helped Unique beat the addiction and get clean.

Ricardo, on the other hand, became the King of The Bean—or so he thought. *"He has 99 problems, but this bitch ain't one"*, thought Unique. One of his 99 was him getting high on his own supply!

Unique took her meds and then returned to her room, where she read her God's Promises book. She focused on one particular part: forgiveness. Her favorites of all were the Bible verses that assured her **God had taken her sins away, as far as the east is to the west; Happy is the person whose sins are forgiven, whose wrongs are pardoned;** and **Happy is the person whom the Lord does not consider guilty and in whom there is nothing false.** She read those passages every morning, noon, and night before going to bed. She also made sure to tell Shein that she was sorry for what she had done.

Just as Unique was getting settled in, there was a knock at her door. It was her counselor, Ms. Barrett. He was Unique's glue. He made sure she didn't relapse and was one of the few who had been with her for the entirety of her stay. Mr. Barrett was 5'9", light-skinned with grey eyes, and the deepest waves in his hair that could sink a ship. Unique couldn't even see that the brother had a crush on her because she was so blinded by her love for Shein.

"How's your day going, Unique?" Mr. Barrett asked.

"One day at a time, right?"

"That's right. That's the way to think! You know your graduation is coming up in two weeks. It will be time for you to go back out into society."

Unique released a silly laugh. *"If society is anything like in here, then I am ready!"*

"Yes, you are ready! You were ready a long time ago. I think you will do well out there. Of course, you will go to a halfway house for six months upon your release. While there, you will live and work. Plus, you will be able to visit your mom whenever you want!" he said encouragingly.

"You know, Mr. Barrett, I'm kind of scared — but I'm ready for whatever comes my way!"

~~~~~~~~~~~

The next morning, Zion was awake but stayed in bed staring at the ceiling. He knew he had to make a move and do it fast. He called his connect in Boston to see what was going on in the city. He also needed to know how Sharmel's business was doing. Before Sharmel got arrested, he had invested his money into a hair salon and barber shop called "Bills." The Feds couldn't touch it. Sharmel knew what he was doing, thanks to Shadow. *"Yo, homie. What's going on in The Bean?"* he asked his connect.

"Man, you already know. It's all good on this end, boss. I wish I could say the same about Spanish Ricardo, though."

Zion let out a little smirk. *"Why? What's going on with him?"*

*"He's being **watched**. That's the word on the street right now."*

"Are you sure?" Zion asked.

*"Believe me when I tell you, boss: He and his soldier have slowed it down a lot. My sales are sky-high, just by putting a little something out there. I mean, I have people coming over the bridge to see **me** for bricks."*

"Okay. I'll be there on Saturday. When I get there, it's straight business. Round up the crew. I'll see y'all at the spot." Zion ended the call and started making plans for his upcoming trip.

~~~~~~~~~~~

Saint was up and ready to go extra early. She didn't want anyone to see her putting the briefcases in the truck's trunk. She shot Zion a quick text to let him know she was on the way. Everyone was still asleep, which was good for her. Majesti must've had company because he was still knocked out, too. She left a note on her mom's dresser, telling her she was going to breakfast with Monae. She then texted Monae, instructing her not to call the house or answer any strange-looking numbers.

When Saint made it to Zion's house, she sat in the car for a while, thinking about the last five years, school, her brothers, and now, Zion. Tears streamed from her eyes and down her cheeks. She just couldn't believe Mykal was back in her life. When one of her favorite songs came on the radio, "Everyone Falls in Love Sometimes" by Beenie Man, she turned up the volume and soaked in every word.

Saint was so lost in the song that the tapping on the window startled her. She jumped as if someone were trying to break into the truck. She wiped her face, turned off the vehicle, got out, and gave Zion the tightest hug ever. They stood in the driveway, hugging for a few moments while she bawled her eyes out.

"What's wrong?!" Zion asked, genuinely concerned.

*"I'm just so tired of all this mess. I don't know if I can continue doing this. Seriously. I want out! This isn't me. What have I gotten myself into? What the hell am I thinking? I'm no dealer. **I'm a college student!**"*

"Saint, calm down. Come into the house, please." She followed Zion inside. *"Listen, first thing's first. I'm going to get you and your mom home safely. I can tell you've had enough of this. You're right: You don't know what you've gotten yourself into, and I won't allow you to continue getting in even deeper."*

"But what about Sharmel?"

"Let me deal with him. I will go see him myself when I make it to The Bean. When you get back to Majesti's, tell your mom that you two will be flying back Friday afternoon. Let Majesti know that you're going home but that he can continue doing what he has to do

for you. If he asks about the loot, let him know that Monae drove it back."

"But she's **not** driving the money back," Saint said, confused.

"I know. I will put half your money in my business accounts from my car dealerships, and some will go into Sharmel's business account. The rest is a surprise."

"A surprise?" Saint asked, feeling a sense of unease overcoming her. *"How are you going to surprise me with **my** money?"* Both laughed.

"Trust me, okay? Trust me. Here are the tickets home for you and your mom. I will be on the next flight after yours and will be staying at the Sheraton on Dalton Street in the Beacon Hill Presidential Suite." He paused to take a deep breath. *"I said it before, and I'm going to say it again: Things are about to get really ugly up there. I need you to stay cool and play innocent and pure. No matter what you hear, I need you to keep a clear head and act like you don't know a thing."*

Saint didn't question Zion whatsoever. She knew enough about "the game" to know when things were about to get ugly. Majesti fucked up, and now he has to pay! *"I feel you,*

Zion. Enough is enough. My family has been through so much. Personally, I am fed up! I thought mom and I would have a normal life after Sharmel and Rein got locked up, but it doesn't seem to be going that way."

*"Saint, you and your mom will have a normal life. Believe it or not, you have lived a normal life. Sharmel made sure he never brought drama to where his family laid their heads. You guys mean the world to him – **especially** you. You are his heart, girl. He would do anything for you, including die."*

"Oh, God! I don't think I could take anybody else dying on me, Zion. The only person I would really love to see dead in that bitch Unique. She is the one who started this whole mess! I have so much anger built up inside of me for that chick. She really doesn't want to cross paths with me."

"Saint, let it go. Believe me: She is being punished. Believe me!" After he spoke those words, he walked away.

~~~~~~~~~~

Friday morning finally came, and Saint and her mother were all packed and ready to pull out at 2:00 p.m. They wanted to be home before the Friday night traffic congested the roads. Monae was going to be waiting for them at the airport to pick them up. Majesti went right along with what Saint decided, clueless as to what was about to hit him. Saint had to giggle to herself. *"He's not as smart as he thinks he is. I see why he hauled ass out of The Bean!"* Zion had set up another drop for Majesti—one that would definitely be a payback…something he would never see coming.

Majesti said his goodbyes to Saint and Ms. Joyce and then went to take care of some business. Before leaving, Saint let Majesti know she would be back the following Saturday to "collect everything." He let her know he would be finished by then and would call to let her know it was all good.

~~~~~~~~~~~

Zion's flight was scheduled to depart at 3:00 p.m. He knew Majesti had four more bricks to get off, so he set up one more drop for two of them. Majesti would be going away for a long time—payback for trying to play Sharmel and stealing from Saint. Majesti knew whom he was supposed to be doing the favor for, so he had to pay for his wrongdoings!

Majesti messed with the **wrong** family!

~~~~~~~~~~~

"*So, are you all packed up and ready to go, Unique?*" asked Mr. Barrett.

"*Packed, yes. Ready to go? No, I am not, but I have no other choice.*"

Mr. Barrett laughed. "*That is so not true! You have choices, Unique. You must be sure to make the good ones. Remember: You have my number, and I can always be reached here. Now, hurry up and say your goodbyes to everyone. Your flight leaves at 2:00 p.m.*"

~~~~~~~~~~

Saint and her mother arrived at the airport and turned in the rental. Saint said her goodbyes to Dai'Sung, gave him a quick hug, and kept it moving.

"*Enjoy your flight, ladies! And Saint, please tell your girl I said what's up!*" Dai'Sung called out.

"*Damn **clown**,*" she thought. "*Okay. I sure will,*" Saint replied with a dismissive wave of her hand.

Once they landed in Boston, the mother-daughter team retrieved their luggage from the baggage claim center and went upstairs to meet Monae. When they reached the top level and stepped outside, Saint couldn't believe her eyes. She saw Unique!

Unique looked at Saint.

Saint looked at Unique.

Were it not for Saint's mother being there, Saint would have killed that bitch on the spot! Fortunately, Saint's mother did not see Unique, even as she began to walk towards Saint.

Unique's mother called out to her. *"Unique! Come on!"*

That happened at the same time Monae called out to Saint. *"Hey, Saint! Let's go, girl!"*

"Oh! There's Monae!" Mama Joyce said.

As both girls walked to their respective rides home, they never took their eyes off each other. If looks could kill, Unique would have been six feet under! Monae saw the interaction and said to Saint, *"It's not worth it, girl. **She's** not worth it."*

On the ride home, everyone was as silent as a sleeping baby. Both Saint and Monae didn't want Mama Joyce to know what just happened.

Mama Joyce broke the silence. *"Are we almost home?"*

"Yes, Mama. We're about ten minutes away," Saint replied.

By 5:00 p.m., they were in the house, getting settled. Mama Joyce took a hot shower that lasted for about 30 minutes. Saint took a shower, too, while Monae laid across Saint's bed, flipping through a magazine. *"Damn, girl! You got a hot date or something? How clean are you trying to get?"* Monae yelled out.

Not a minute later, Saint exited the bathroom with a towel wrapped around her and another around her hair. *"Girl, shut up! I had to wash my hair. Believe it or not, they didn't have my hair products down there! I couldn't believe it, Mo! What I also couldn't believe was that trick was going to walk right up on me at the airport!"*

"I wonder what she wanted to say," said Monae.

"That bitch has nothing to say to me! There's nothing that could come out of her mouth that would change a thing. Nothing! She's lucky Mama was with me, or else she would have gotten the beatdown of the year! I heard she wasn't doing well."

"She looked damn good to me," replied Monae with a shoulder shrug.

"Yeah. She's probably been in rehab for a few years, getting herself cleaned up. You know what, though? I don't really give a rat's

ass! I swear: If I see her again, I don't know what I will do! I swear: I just don't know!" Saint's rant was interrupted by a call from Zion. *"Hello?"* she said with bitterness in her voice.

"Damn, girl! What's wrong? Something sounds wrong."

"Nothing!" Saint yelled into the phone before throwing it onto the bed and storming into the bathroom.

Monae picked up the phone to talk to Zion. *"Hey, Zion!"*

"Who's this?"

"Monae."

"Oh. Hey, Monae. What's going on with Saint?"

"Well, where should I start?"

"Cut the bull, Monae."

"Saint bumped into Unique today at the airport."

"What? What happened?" Zion asked in a panic.

"Nothing happened. Unique started walking up to Saint, but her mother called her, so she changed her mind."

"May I please speak with her? Please?" begged Zion. *"I really don't need her doing anything crazy."*

"I know what you mean. She is very upset right now. I don't know if I should leave her here. Her mom's resting. I really don't know what to do!"

"Listen. I'm in town now. She knows that. If she wants to come and chill, would you bring her? I really don't want her driving anywhere when she's that upset," Zion explained.

"I'll give her the phone. If she wants to come to you, I will bring her. If she doesn't, then you will have to come and play babysitter. I have kids of my own to get back home to, aight?"

"Yeah. Aight."

"Hold on, Zion." Monae walked into the bathroom, handed Saint the phone, and went downstairs.

~~~~~~~~~~

"Hello?"

"You okay, Saint?"

"Yes, I'm fine."

"Saint, don't let Unique get you out of character. You're better than that."

"I know, Zion, but just seeing her brought back a flood of unhappy memories. I blame her for everything that has happened." Saint was in tears again. All Zion could do was listen without interruption. He let her pour her heart out, knowing she never came to grips with Shein's death nor that of her father.

"Hey, why don't you come to the hotel so that we can grab a bite to eat?" Zion suggested. *"We can just chill and catch up on things. Would you like that?"*

"Yes, I would," she said in between sobs.

"Do you want me to come to pick you up?"

"Yes, please. I really don't want to drive, and Monae will be leaving soon."

"Okay. Give me an hour. I'll see you then."

~~~~~~~~~~

Meanwhile, back in the ATL...

Dai'Sung was preparing for his vacation, but before he went anywhere, he had to take care of some business. He called Majesti to see if it was okay to give Nazen his cell and to let him know that Nazen just might need another drop.

"I'm alright with that," Majesti stated. The only thing he was concerned about was dollar-dollar bills, y'all! "Damn! He already got rid of that last brick?"

"Yeah, dawg! Nazen is the man where he's from. He's doing big things in Phoenix."

"Okay! Well, that's cool, D. Tell him to get at me when he's ready. As a matter of fact, tell him I will give him a good deal on these last four bricks: $25 grand each."

"Whoa! You're letting them go for that?!" Dai'Sung asked, stunned.

"Dude, I want these out of my presence. I have bigger and better things to do and bigger and better fish to fry! So, when are you pulling out for your vacation? Are you going anywhere special?"

"Yeah. I'm taking my mom and sister to Cancun for the week. It's my sister's birthday weekend. We're leaving on Saturday."

"That's cool. Well, leave my cell with that dude and tell him to hit me up when he's ready," Majesti instructed.

"No doubt. See you when I get back," said Dai'Sung.

Majesti had **no** idea what was coming for him. When you don't play by the rules, you **will** lose "the game."

Stay tuned for the thrilling continuation of this series...

MASK OFF: Orders From Zion

Mask Off: Two Faces